AWAKENING
OF A
SOUL KEEPER

BRIENNE DUBH

PREQUEL TO THE SOUL KEEPER SERIES

For my daughters.

My little chicken and little turtle I love you both so much.

Thank you for always keeping me on my toes and for the never-ending supply of hugs & kisses.

Also, a huge thank you to my beta readers for their honesty and encouragement.

Contents

PROLOGUE

Isaac closed his eyes and called out once more. He opened them and looked at his mobile phone. It was on silent, flashing, and still just out of reach. He knew exactly who was calling but didn't have any strength left to crawl across the graveled path to answer it. Everything around him was moving in slow motion, or maybe it just seemed that way.

He wondered if this was what happened when one was close to their end. It was almost funny to him that this was it. After all this time and everything he'd seen, done and been through, he was going to die like this, behind a crappy cinema complex in a pool of his own blood and ash.

As another of his men fell lifelessly beside him, he wondered how someone had managed to get the drop on him. It would have taken a lot to plan and execute an ambush like this. There weren't many left who had the balls to challenge, never mind get the better of him. Yet here he was beaten, broken and butchered. Blindsided.

He felt blood spray across his face as another of

his men took a hit and went down. Kali. He was still alive but from the looks of it, he didn't have long left either. Kali's face was a mask of rage and pain. Looking every bit the warrior he once was.

Isaac gave him a resigned smile and Kali scowled back at him. They both knew that if he and Kali were down, then the others would not survive this night.

It was almost too easy how he and his men were being taken down. The strength of their attackers was astounding. He was outraged and annoyed that he would die like this, not knowing how it happened. Although after fighting with one who had managed to get the better of him, he had his suspicions.

"Make sure you kill them all." He heard one of the attackers say in a raspy voice. He thought the man had an accent, but in his beaten state, he just couldn't place it.

He didn't know how long he had left but one thing he knew with absolute certainty was that every one of them would pay. His men were strong, good and loyal, and it pained him that they were being massacred simply because they were with him. But there was simply nothing more he could do.

His phone was still flashing, but his body felt as though it was made of lead. He was fading fast and his vision started to blur just as a large figure loomed above him, wielding a sharp and bloody sword.

This was it.

He took a deep shuddering breath and closed his

eyes, focusing all his remaining energy, enough to reach out with his mind one last time.

It's time. Either death or darkness will claim me. Avenge me, brothers!

Isaac caught the sound of wings flapping followed by a loud roar.

Bjorn!

Then, darkness.

CHAPTER ONE

"Teddy! Teddy where are you?" Sam shouted into the living room, then into the kitchen as he rushed into the house.

"Up here."

Strands of her long dark hair fell from the loose bun on top of her head as Theodora sprawled across the bed in her pajamas, scrolling through her laptop. She had been working all morning, hoping to finish a commercial script before the weekend.

As she read through her work, she smiled and nodded approvingly at the screen. She knew it was good. She enjoyed working as a copywriter on marketing media, especially for Stroupe, a prestigious theatre company which ran an outreach programme for youths with disabilities. This particular company always paid well, but she'd been flat out over the last few weeks and was looking forward to handing it in and taking a break.

Sam came through the bedroom door with a huge grin on his face. Even after all this time together, his breath still caught when he looked at her. Every day, he thought back and wondered how on earth he'd managed not only to catch her eye, but also found the nerve to talk to her after she gave him that heart stopping smile of hers.

He watched as she bit down on her bottom lip, full and naturally red, and his smile widened. It was a habit of hers that he would never tire of watching.

"Someone's in a good mood." Theodora beamed up at Sam.

He was still dressed in his work suit, but he'd undone the top buttons of his white shirt and loosened his tie. He had obviously been running a hand through his short black hair as it had lost the just styled look he'd left with that morning.

She loved it when he looked like that.

With his ruffled hair, and salt and pepper stubble coming through, she had often told Sam he reminded her of the actor who played the playboy billionaire scientist in her favourite superheroes movies. He always laughed as he considered himself less of a superhero and more of a nerd.

"Guess who was just assigned as the new auditor for NocLife Leisure?" Sam smiled smugly as he sat down next to Theodora and began taking off his jacket and tie.

"Seriously?" She gasped.

"Yep." Sam grinned.

"Well done, babe." She leaned across and gave him a peck on the lips. "That's amazing news. Does this mean you'll get a raise? Actually, forget money. Does it mean you'll get to meet the big boss?"

"The elusive Mr Pierce. I doubt it. Apart from Mr Montgomery, I don't think any of the people who work for him knows what he looks like. That's the rumor anyway."

"That's just crazy. I wonder why he's the only one who's seen him. Oh, I know, Pierce is probably like Bruce Wayne. All broody with a tragic secret past that keeps him in hiding, and Montgomery is his version of Alfred. Or he's scarred from some horrible accident, which is why no one has ever seen his face. Like the phantom of the opera." She gushed out her thoughts as usual making Sam smile.

"Phantom? Bruce Wayne? Seriously. What is it with you and these comic book men. Sorry to burst your bubble, but I think the only thing he has in common with Bruce Wayne is the obscene money he has. And I'm sorry to shoot another hole in your theory, but he's at least a multi-billionaire. So *if* he were horribly disfigured, he'd probably have the best surgeons money could buy come to his house, fix him up in his bedroom and be on the cover of GQ before you could say handsome bachelor. I can already see the wheels turning in that head of yours, Teddy. All the wild ideas running around up there. You're hoping he turns out to be like one of your book boyfriends." Sam teased.

"It's comic book *boyfriend*, and there is only one.

Thor and I are exclusive these days."

"You're crazy, you know that, right?"

"Yep!" Theodora grinned.

"Look. I just don't want you getting all excited thinking I'll get to meet him. So don't go getting your hopes up"

"I won't. Wait, I bet he's an eighty-year-old recluse with a huge house and lots of dogs."

"So now you think my new boss, entrepreneur Lyzander Pierce, is the old man version of the cat lady?"

"I like that." Theodora nodded. "Instead of Batman, Lyzander Pierce is Catman."

"Really?" Sam tried to hold back his laughter as he listened to his wife ramble on.

"Ooh, even better, what if he is actually a she? Dun dun duuuun."

Sam couldn't help but laugh out loud at her dramatic revelation sound effect.

Theodora continued on, talking over him. "What if Lyzander is actually a Laura or Lucy? You could be working for crazy old Lilly Pierce and never know it. I mean no one has ever really seen 'the guy', have they?" She gasped, making the air quotes.

"You. Are. Crazy!" Sam chuckled while leaning down to take off his shoes and socks.

"I'm nuts, baby, but that's why you love me. And I love you because you're sexy." She pulled him back up for a kiss. "You're smart." She continued to kiss him after each reason she gave. "– and funny. And now you're a big shot auditor for one of the biggest names in entertainment."

"I don't think the words big shot and auditor go together."

"They do when it's about you. You're amazing with numbers and figures. I'd suck at your job."

"I know which figure I'd like to work on right now," Sam drawled as he slowly moved his hands towards her in a playful manner.

She slapped them away. "Hands off, buddy. No distractions. Genius at work here." She waved her hands over her work area.

"I've been trying for so long to get one of the big accounts, but I can't believe I got *them*."

"You must have really impressed some of the higher ups."

"It had to have been Prichard. I'm glad he finally sees my worth. I start auditing them on Monday, and I'll be working out of their London office."

"London." Theodora groaned loudly and threw her hands up, looking very unimpressed.

"Yeah, and I was thinking maybe you'd want to come with me," Sam hedged.

"Why does it have to be London?" Theodora groused.

"What's wrong with London?"

"Nothing, it's just that I could really use some sun." She sat up and swung her legs over the edge of the bed to inspect her skin.

"Teddy, you don't need any sun," Sam eyed her naturally olive skin.

"I didn't say I needed it, silly. I just really miss it. I know I should be used to it by now, but your horrible English weather is killing me." She teased with a playful pout, bumping shoulders with him.

"So, it's my weather now?" Sam raised an eyebrow at her.

"It is when it rains like this. And as much as I love living in Manchester, it seems to rain more here than anywhere else in the country. Or the whole damn world actually." Theodora mumbled, gesturing over to the window.

It was only just after midday but it was wet, dark and ominous outside, as though something bad was on its way.

"I'm just saying, it would have been nice if you got assigned somewhere like France. We could have gone to Paris or California. We could have stayed with mom." She sighed dreamily.

"Well, I'm sorry my promotion doesn't meet your high standards, Missy," Sam said jokingly and bumped her back.

"Why couldn't it have been the LA office? It's been so long since I saw my old friends." Theodora sighed.

"Firstly, you've been to France loads of times. And as for LA, you always get bored when you go back home. You argue with your mother, then tell me you're ready to come back within hours of getting there."

"Okay, so you might have a point about my mother. But not about France. I may have been there lots of times, but not Paris. It would have been cool to stay in the city of love with my husband. I'm just saying, NocLife have clubs and casinos all over the world. But you get the London office two hours down the road."

"Ungrateful woman, do you want to come or not?" Sam grabbed a pillow and hit her in the face, knocking her back onto the bed.

"Yes please." Theodora laughed from underneath the pillow.

"We can get a train this afternoon from Piccadilly and book a nice hotel. By the time we get there, it will be too late to do much of anything, but we can spend the next two days doing all the touristy things you're always going on about. Then I was thinking on Friday, we could check out one of the NocLife clubs. There's one not far from Soho called The Veil. I can enjoy the club before I have to be there in work mode. What do you think?"

"Sounds like fun."

"We could go dancing." Sam laid down.

"It's been ages since we went out dancing," Theodora sighed.

"And maybe get something to eat," he added

cautiously.

"Ooh, Soho Sushi here I come,"

"I was thinking more like room service, not restaurants. It's been ages since we did something else as well," Sam rested his hand on her stomach and moved it lower.

Theodora sat up immediately, displacing his hand. She didn't know what to say. She loved Sam, but she hadn't felt at all sexually attracted to him for some time.

Not since the miscarriage.

They hadn't known she was pregnant. Three or four weeks along, the doctors had called it a chemical pregnancy. They hadn't planned it. She didn't even know she was pregnant until she wasn't, but it still left her feeling hollow.

She had thought that was the only reason she felt this way towards Sam. But as the weeks went on, she realised it wasn't just that. It was something else entirely, but she couldn't figure out what it was. Everything would be amazing between them, but when he touched her, she'd go cold. She couldn't understand why. In her mind, she wanted to try to be with him that way, but the touch which used to excite her, now left her cold and uncomfortable.

They stayed in an awkward silence for some time.

"Sam, you know it's not you. I just...after what happened...I'm still not ready." She hated using that as the excuse. It was a partial truth, but she didn't know what else to tell him.

"I know, Teddy. I didn't mean to push...but...it's been months since we–"

"I know," Theodora cut him off.

"I'm not saying we should try for another baby, but we need to move forward. We need to reconnect." Sam sat up and took her hand in his.

"I know. I'll try," she whispered.

"That's all I'm asking. You're not mad?"

"No, not at all." She bumped his shoulder.

He retaliated by going for the ticklish spot on her side.

She squealed and slapped his hands away, leaving them both laughing.

"So does that mean you're coming to London with me?"

"If I can get this piece in before we go, I'll have the next ten days off."

"Do you have much to do?"

"This is my final read through. Then I can send it off to the client. Just give me thirty minutes to finish this off and I'll start packing."

"London here we come." Sam kissed the back of her hand before leaving her to her work.

* * * *

"This place is packed," Theodora shouted over the loud music blaring from the speakers above them.

"No wonder they make so much money."

Sam had found them a table in a corner close to the bar. There was a constant flow of people coming and going with drinks, but she was just relieved to have a seat. They had been dancing non-stop for at least an hour, and although she felt like one of the older ones in a young crowd, she loved the music and just wanted to dance.

She couldn't put her finger on it but there was something about this club, The Veil, that made her feel free. *Probably the booze*, she thought.

"So, what do you think of the place?"

"It's a good business. Seems well run, a real money spinner," Sam replied stiffly.

Theodora laughed. "So much for saving work mode for Monday," she teased.

"I like the place. It's just not my usual scene that's all."

"I'm not sure what my scene is anymore, but I'm loving it. This place is huge. Did you see the upper level?"

"That's where the VIPs go," Sam commented.

"Really? Well, we can go up there next time. I'm enjoying this level far too much," She joked.

"Never mind the VIP section. I think I'm ready for the OAP section." Sam glanced around at the younger crowd.

"My god, it's so hot in here," Theodora groused as she picked up a beer mat and fanned herself.

"Do you want to go outside and get some air?"

"Yeah, but let's get a drink first. I'm thirsty as hell." Sam leaned in and she kissed him gently.

Theodora laughed to herself as he walked away. He was now wearing her red lipstick, but she wasn't planning on saying anything to him about it until much later.

One beer and a shot of Tequila later, she had all but forgotten about going outside. She was ready to dance. She laughed as she dragged her reluctant husband onto the dance floor. She closed her eyes, enjoying the euphoric feeling that washed over her.

She felt hands on her hips, and then the press of a body that wasn't Sam's mold into her back.

"Dance with me."

She opened her eyes and turned to find a very drunk young woman, who was trying to ignore the advances of an even drunker man, who seemed to be doing some sort of acrobatics to entice them.

"Dance with me please," the girl begged. "I lost my friends and this guy won't leave me alone."

The girl seemed more annoyed than worried before Teddy nodded and pulled the girl into her.

Sam smiled then gestured toward the table and his feet.

She knew he was getting tired, so she nodded back and he left them to it.

They danced to a few more songs before the guy finally got the hint and disappeared. A few songs later, the girl's friends showed up next to them and dragged her off to the bar for shots to thank her for rescuing their friend.

As the girls waited at the bar for their drinks to arrive, she shouted over to Sam. "Are you okay?"

"Yeah, I'm fine. Just enjoying the show." He shook his head as one of the girls placed a shot in front of her.

"You don't mind, do you?"

"Not at all. Have fun."

"I am," Theodora announced with a beaming smile before turning and did her shot with her new friends.

She was just about ready for another dance when she started to feel very strange. At first, she thought it was the shot. But for some bizarre reason, she knew it had nothing to do with the alcohol. It was as though she was being pulled from the inside out. Her breathing picked up and she knew she had to get out of there.

"Are you okay?" Sam shouted over.

"Yeah, I just need the bathroom and some air."

"Do you want me to come with you?"

She shook her head. "No, you stay there. I'll be back soon."

She didn't wait for a response as she turned and made her way across the dance floor. She didn't want to freak him out, but something was really wrong. Although wrong wasn't exactly how she felt. Her breathing was harsh now, and though she was worried, she felt an unexpected wave of excitement wash over her.

She pushed her way through the hordes of people on the dance floor until she came to the mile long queue for the bathroom. She was about to get in line when, as if on autopilot, she turned and walked away in the opposite direction towards the back of the club. She came to a staff-only corridor but it felt like the right direction to go. Straight ahead, at the end of the corridor, was what looked to be a door to an office. But before that, on her left, was a door with a sign that said 'staff bathroom'.

"Oh, screw it," Theodora muttered and shoved through the doors as though she was being chased.

Thankfully, the bathroom was empty and no one saw her fall into the sink. She ran the cold water and splashed it onto her face and neck. She felt warm and tingly, but she knew it had nothing to do with alcohol or the heat of the club.

The tugging was still there but it was different. It no longer felt like she was being pulled somewhere. But rather, something was tugging inside of her. The film *Aliens* flashed into her mind and, although she knew it was ridiculous, she panicked, thinking something was trying to tear its way out of her.

"What in the hell is wrong with me?" She huffed to her reflection as she splashed more water.

Apart from her dark brown eyes being the size of

saucers, she didn't look any different. Her reflection was normal; she was dressed in a casual black vest top and skinny jeans with her long brown hair hanging just below her breast. But she was a mess on the inside. It felt like a tornado was twisting its way around her body. Her heart was pounding against her ribcage and she could hear it getting louder and louder.

"I'm too young to have a heart attack," she exclaimed as she held onto the sink and tried to breathe steadily.

The beating of her heart picked up again to a scary pace, and so did the volume in her head.

Then, after what felt like hours, it all abruptly stopped.

The room was silent, apart from the sound of her heavy breathing.

She placed a hand on her chest. Her heartbeat was normal once more. The tugging now felt like a pulse. There was something inside her, warm and pulsing.

"What the hell is that?" She moved away until her back hit the wall and slid down into a sitting position. "Okay, Theodora. Deep breaths. Take a minute, get your shit together, get Sam and get the hell out of here."

She placed her head between her legs and took several deep breaths but nothing got better.

Maybe I'll take five minutes, she thought as she

continued to slowly breath in and out.

CHAPTER TWO

Lyzander peered across the dark room as the electronic beat pumped and the strobe lights crisscrossed, bringing the heaving dance floor to life.

The scent of alcohol, perfume, sweat and lust filled the air. Normally, that cocktail of scents pointed towards a packed club, which meant more money in his bank account, and this usually eased whatever bad mood he was in.

But not tonight.

Although he was dressed simply in jeans and a dark collarless shirt and should have blended in, his unusual looks caught the eye of more than a few patrons as he strode across the dance floor. To most, he looked to be in his mid to late thirties with an intimidating demeanor of a General about to go to war.

Though Lyzander was a good-looking man, he was scary looking too. Being over six feet four, he naturally stood out. But it was his fair skin paired with his white blonde hair that hung halfway down his back that made him even more noticeable.

Thankfully the club lighting only made him look pale, and not the colour that his skin actually was.

Not that anyone would remember how he looked when they left.

Every house, business and pretty much everything he owned had heavy protections placed on them by a powerful caster friend of his.

No human would ever remember seeing him.

Lyzander's head snapped to the side when he caught the scent of blood. His eyes locked onto a table where a group of women were doing shots and slamming the shot glasses back down onto the table. One of the women had obviously slammed hers too hard as the glass broke, cutting her palm and causing her blood to pour from the wound.

He found this worrying. Not because he found the sight disturbing, but because he didn't long to grab hold of the woman and drink her dry.

It had been too long for him, and his kind needed sustenance on a regular basis just as humans did. He should be ravenous, unable to keep himself from feasting on the dancing bags of plasma. But for some reason, the rich aroma of her blood wasn't doing a thing for him. It only made him angry and more anxious than he already was. With everything that was happening, he couldn't afford to show weakness of any kind.

He turned away and brushed past desperate men pouring over scantily clad sweaty women as he made his way towards the back of the club where his office was. Tonight, he didn't care about how busy they were or how much money he made. He didn't care if the place burned to the ground either.

Tonight, he only had one thing on his mind.

"Find me someone to kill," he demanded as he slammed the door shut behind him and began to pace.

"You know we don't do that anymore," Roman replied from across the room.

Dressed in a grey three-piece suit, Roman was perched elegantly on the edge of a black leather recliner, watching the on-goings in the club via several monitors.

"I want to rip somebody's head off," Lyzander stated in the detached manner of one who had done it many times before. "I need to tear into quivering flesh."

Roman turned to face Lyzander and could see pain and rage coming off him in waves. Lyzander was awoken when Graven had cried out to him. They had attacked there first but had seriously underestimated his strength. They'd both tried calling Isaac's phone but it kept ringing with no answer. Graven contacted Bjorn the dragon shifter as backup since neither of them could get to him. As Lyzander was about to call out to Isaac they heard their brother's broken voice in their mind.

Avenge me Brothers!

Those were the last words he heard Isaac say.

"You will. We'll find out who did this to Isaac, and then you can rip and tear away at them. Slowly. But I can't have you killing an innocent and having that on your conscience."

"I have no conscience, Roman," Lyzander stated blandly.

"Which is why I've been acting as yours all these years. I'm also your friend, and friends don't let friends kill when they're in a bad mood."

"You are also my employee and paid to do what I say. So go get me someone to kill."

"No."

"Yes. I'm not paying you to argue with me."

"Maybe you should pay me more."

"Maybe I should sack you again!" Lyzander huffed.

"Maybe if you stopped sacking me every time you get pissed off, I'd take that threat more seriously."

Lyzander stopped in front of the monitors and watched the club for a few minutes before he made his way over to his desk and sat down.

Roman frowned as he watched him rest his forehead against the table. Something wasn't right with Lyzander. They'd known each other for centuries, and Lyzander was always calm and calculated, amongst other things. This was new. It was the first time Roman has seen him anxious and restless.

"What's wrong with you?"

"What do you think is wrong? In the last twenty-four hours, someone tried to kill Graven and Isaac, and my home has been burned to the ground. This is why I don't trust people. Thank god only you knew I was coming here. How the hell did they even find out about that place?"

"Someone is trying to take down the council," Roman remarked.

"Someone with inside information."

"If only Graven hadn't lost his cool and taken all the assassins out, we'd have a lead now. Not that I blame him. I'd probably have done the same."

"Isaac had to go straight into a healing sleep. It could be weeks before he's able to tell us anything. Though some of his attackers were stupid enough to carry ID on them, so at least that's somewhere to start.

"Thank goodness Bjorn showed up when he did. He's taken care of the bodies in LA and will look after the business until Isaac has recovered. Calvin is doing the same in Melbourne, though Graven wasn't too happy at being told to go to ground."

"I can imagine but tell Bjorn I want him here. Leo can take care of LA, he is more than capable. I have a feeling I will need Bjorn with me."

"Of course. Oh good, Michael has arrived." Roman said with faux enthusiasm as he glanced at one of the screens.

Lyzander shook his head slowly and groaned.

"I still don't understand why you saved him from those human hunters. He's a sadistic and vicious dog. If you dislike him so much, why use him?" Roman inquired.

"He may be a dog, but he's been an extremely loyal, vicious and sadistic dog. He isn't restricted to the night like we are, and I know he'll get the job done. If there is anything worth knowing, he will find out. We *have* to find them, Roman. No one has ever gotten this close to us before." Lyzander raised his head and rubbed his eyes. "I can't believe we have nothing on them yet."

"It's been one day, Lyzander. Give it time. You're tired and frustrated, and I haven't seen you with a donor in a while. When was the last time you fed?"

Lyzander took a deep breath. He didn't want Roman fussing. He hadn't told him anything before and wasn't keen now but he answered. "Three days ago."

"What the hell, Ly. Are you trying to kill yourself? You need blood."

"I haven't felt the need to feed –"

"You haven't felt the need?" Roman interrupted, taken aback.

"I know." He sighed. "Something is very wrong, but I will deal with it later. We have more important things to sort out."

"More important? Are you insane? Nothing is

more important than you, especially not now. We need you to be strong."

"I am strong, Roman. Never doubt that," Lyzander stated in an ice-cold tone which would have terrified anyone else.

But Roman knew him well enough.

"I never have, and I never will doubt you, Meus rex. I just want...we all need for you to be well." A knock at the door interrupted them. "That will be Michael."

Lyzander watched as Roman stood and walked over to the door, his gait slow and refined. Roman was a combination of grace, power and wisdom. In some ways, he was closer to him than he was his brothers. Roman nagged like an old woman, but he was always there.

Feeling unsettled and unsure for the first time in his long life, he'd never needed Roman more.

"Roman, why did you call me that? Meus rex. It's been hundreds of years since anyone has used that term."

"It just...felt right. But you have always been my king."

Hearing this unsettled Lyzander even more.

"Thank you, my friend. I'll feed later, Roman, you have my word."

Roman nodded and opened the door.

Michael was leaning against the door frame and smiled when he caught sight of Roman. "Leech," he greeted.

"Shifty," Roman replied.

Michael was a shifter and a dodgy one at that. There was no love lost between them and he hated Roman's little nickname for him, which is why Roman used it.

Michael had a slight European accent and looked to be in in thirties, though he was probably much older. No one knew his real age or where he was from. Dressed in a navy suit with his black hair cut short, showing off his square jawline, he could have been mistaken for an accountant or a doctor. However, he had an air about him that screamed evil.

Michael straightened up and bumped shoulders with Roman as he entered the office. He may as well have walked into a six-foot brick wall since Roman was just as hard and didn't move an inch. They squared up to each other and Michael smiled, opening his mouth and licking a fang he'd let drop down.

"Go ahead, fido. You know I'd love an excuse to put you down."

There were many kinds of shifters and Michael was a dog shifter, if you could call it that. He turned into a giant beast, which looked like the offspring of a Rottweiler who'd mated with a hellhound. He was scary in human form but terrifying as his beast.

"Fido, that's so old but actually quite funny for

you, old man. But do you know what would really make me laugh? Ripping that smug head off your pretentious shoulders."

"Enough." Lyzander commanded, his voice barely above a whisper but they both heard him.

Roman closed and then leaned against the door.

Michael turned his back on him and walked over to the desk.

One was either fearless or insane to turn their back on a vampire. Roman guessed he was a little of both.

"Lyzander Pierce. You called and I answered. What can I do for you on this fine evening?" Michael greeted happily.

"I need you to do what you do best."

"What I do best? Huh, that could be a lot of different things. Kill, maim, torture. You'll have to be a bit more specific," he said playfully.

"In the last twenty-four hours, someone has tried to kill my brothers and burnt my house in France to the ground, which I believe was also an attempt on my life."

Michael's face dropped at his words. "Are they ok?" He asked with genuine concern.

"Graven is fine."

"And Isaac?"

"He will be...with time."

"I see. You want me to do it all then?"

Lyzander was quiet for a moment before he stood

and slowly walked around the desk to stand in front of Michael.

"Michael, as you know, I trust very few people and only a handful of those are not vampire." He locked eyes with Michael meaningfully. "I need you to go to France for me. I want you to take care of my interests there indefinitely. I want you to find out who torched my house, question them and then punish them. Find out what they know, who ordered the hit on me and my brothers, and where I can find them. I need you to get your hands dirty with this one. So, yes. Maim, kill, do whatever is necessary by any means necessary. Specifically, I need you to be the sadistic animal I alone know you are. Will you do this for me?"

"With pleasure," Michael bowed.

"Good. I'll have you on a flight in two hours. In the meantime, feel free to enjoy the club. Just don't cause any trouble."

"I can promise you many things, Lyzander, but that isn't one of them." Michael gave him a small nod before he turned back towards the door.

Roman stood straight and opened the door but not enough for him to get through.

Michael looked over at Roman and was surprised when he gave him a nod of approval before opening the door wider.

Roman didn't like the rogue shifter, but he respected his loyalty to Lyzander.

Michael gave him a nod in return and left.

"I saw that," Lyzander remarked. "So, you two can play nicely."

His tone hadn't changed but Roman knew he was teasing him. "Oh, be quiet." He took a seat back in front of the monitors. "Go find a nice girl and convince her to donate some blood. Hopefully that will rid you of this surliness."

"I doubt it, but I really do need to get out of here. I'll be out front."

* * * *

Theodora wasn't sure how long she had been sitting there for, and even though she was still wobbly, she knew she had to get out of the bathrooms. The pulsing was getting stronger and somehow, she knew something big was coming.

She stood up, grabbed some paper towels from the dispenser and blotted her face. Taking a few deep breaths, she opened the door and stepped out into the corridor. Unfortunately, straight into a large figure.

"I'm so sorry," She said, thinking she'd been caught coming out of the staff toilets by an employee.

But when she looked up, it was into the face of evil. He was tall with dark hair, dressed in a dark suit. He was actually normal looking, apart from the malevolent look in his eyes.

Instinctively, her body shivered and every cell in her body told her she was in trouble and needed to get away. She took a step to the left to pass him, but he took a step in the same direction and blocked her. Stepping to the other side, he followed her move, blocking her again.

"Where are you going? You might be sorry, but I didn't say you were forgiven," He warned in a tone that scared the heck out her.

"I'm sorry. I didn't see you, it was an accident. Please move out of my way so I can get back to my husband."

"I don't think I will."

"Excuse me?"

"I was hoping to find someone to keep me company for a few hours, and you more than fit my requirements." He looked her up and down.

He took a step forward and she took a step back, which unfortunately brought her back up against a wall. The man reached out as though he was going to grab her.

"Don't touch me," she hissed angrily but he smiled as his hand got closer. "I'm warning you."

He didn't listen.

Repulsed when his hand brushed her jaw as he fingered a lock of her hair, Theodora reacted instinctively and punched him in the face. She moved to run as he stumbled but his huge frame blocked her off once again. With one hand, he grabbed her by the throat and lifted her off the floor, holding her against the wall. When she looked down, the man had a cruel smile on his bloody lips.

"Now why would you go and do a thing like that. I was only playing with you. But that actually hurt me. How did a little thing like you manage that?"

"Put me down!" She rasped out and his hand faltered.

A brief look of surprise flashed across his face before a smile took its place. "Oh my, you are intriguing. Yes, you will do nicely," he chuckled darkly as she struggled.

Theodora desperately tried to think of ways to get away but she could barely concentrate. Not because her hand was hurting from the punch she'd thrown, or because she was being attacked by the creepy banker with superhuman strength. But because the pulsing inside her suddenly grew so intense she could hardly focus.

Just as she moved preparing to kick the guy and separate his balls from his body, the pressure of his hand at her throat vanished and she dropped ungracefully to the floor. After coughing and spluttering for a few seconds, she looked across to one end of the corridor and saw the banker dude in a crumpled heap on the ground. He groaned and swore a couple of times before rolling and standing up faster than was humanly possible.

"What the h-" She stopped talking when she felt

a presence beside her.

She turned and looked up at the most beautiful yet terrifying sight she had ever seen.

A tall man stood before her, staring in the direction of the banker dude he had just thrown. Only this wasn't a man at all. He could have been an angel with his handsome face, azure eyes and long, almost white hair flowing around him.

But she knew he wasn't.

It wasn't his pale skin or the inhumane snarling that gave it away either. It was the long, sharp pointy fangs in his mouth and the deadly look on his face.

"Never lay your hands on her again."

Even though he hadn't raised his voice, it was so cold no one could have missed his deadly intent.

"Do you understand me, Michael?"

"I didn't realise she was claimed," he explained but when nothing more was said, he simply nodded and slunk away.

Theodora released the breath she didn't know she had been holding. She felt light headed, her heart was beating out of her chest, and the strong pulsing hadn't eased either. If anything, it seemed to grow even more frantic. The tall man, her savior, looked down at her and took a step closer. She thought he was angry with her, but then his head dropped to the side and he seemed puzzled as he studied her.

"What are you?" He rumbled, his baritone voice

confusing her.

"What am I? What are you?" She frowned slightly.

The man looked taken aback by her sass and was about to speak when another man suddenly appeared outside the office door.

"I can't leave you alone for a minute," the man shook his head, a little amused at the situation he'd walked in on. But that quickly changed to annoyed. "Fangs, Lyzander," he admonished.

"Lyzander? You are Lyzander Pierce?" Theodora asked in amazement.

Lyzander hadn't taken his eyes off the little thing before him, but he retracted his fangs before he spoke. "How do you know me?"

"I don't. I mean, I know who you are. As in I've heard of you. I mean everyone has heard of you. But I've never met you before. We've never met. I didn't know what you looked like until just now. I didn't even know who you were until he said your name. I thought you were a cat lady or Bruce Wayne," she babbled away.

Lyzander studied her for another moment before offering her his hand.

Theodora's head spun, her heart was racing and her body was pulsing. Taking stock of the situation, she realized she'd been attacked by some sort of monster, only to be saved by this thing in front of her. A creature now offering her a helping hand, a man named Lyzander Pierce.

She was terrified, but strangely enough, she also felt compelled. Taking a deep breath, she reached out and placed her hand in his.

The second their hands touched, everything changed.

Their hands locked and neither could let go. Panic flashed across their faces but they were incapable of doing anything.

They both felt it.

Something powerful and fast flowed from her to him, like wild rushing waters cascading over a waterfall. Just as quick, the feeling changed to a static electric shock, but a thousand times stronger.

Theodora felt as though energy was being ripped from her body. Lyzander grunted as though he had been punched in the chest at the same moment she cried out in pain as a burning sensation washed over the right side of her body.

The whole episode only lasted seconds before Lyzander jerked his hand away as though it was on fire. He stumbled backwards, staring accusingly at her, before he stormed down the corridor, past his friend, and into the office.

The pulsing has stopped but she now had something else to worry about.

It now tingled where the burning pain had been. She knew two things without a doubt. Firstly, something was etched into her skin. She just knew it, like the way her body knew just how to breathe. Secondly, she was now unequivocally connected to this man. This creature. Lyzander.

Her body wobbled but strong hands caught her before she fell.

"Are you alright?"

Theodora had long forgotten about the other man. She gasped and went to move away but she had no strength in her legs.

"Easy now. That was quite a jolt you took."

"Who are you? And what do you want?" She rasped out.

"My name is Roman Montgomery. I'm the manager here. I just want to help you."

"You saw him. What the hell is he?" She demanded.

"Why don't you come with me and we'll talk? I'll explain everything."

She shook her head. "I don't think so, buddy. You knew he had fangs! I'm not going anywhere with you."

"Yes, you're right. I did know, and I know you're in pain too, down your right side. Let me guess, just below your ear down your neck, along your breast, arm and side to your thigh? How am I doing?"

Theodora frowned. "How could you know that? Do you know what just happened to me...to us?"

"I think I do. May I?" Roman reached over to turn her head. He spoke soothingly when she flinched at his movement. "Please don't be afraid of me. I won't hurt you, and if I'm right..." He trailed off as she allowed him to turn her head and gently touched behind her ear.

He gasped before whispering, "Regina."

"What? What is it? What was that? German?"

"Latin. I know what's happening, and I will happily tell you everything. But not here. Let's go into my office and -"

"No! He's in there." Theodora shook her head feverously.

Roman gave her a reassuring smile. "He won't hurt you. Trust me on this."

She eyed him skeptically. "I don't know you."

"Look at me. Really look at me, and you will know if you can trust me or not."

Theodora took a step back and eyed the man before her. Before she had really thought about it, she found herself nodding. But as he started to move, she stopped him.

"My husband is waiting for me by the bar."

"You're married?" Roman's brows furrowed.

"Yes."

"Shit," he cursed silently under his breath. "How long have you been together?

"Five years."

"And married?"

"A year. Why?"

"Do you live here? In London."

"No."

"You came here about three days ago, didn't you?"

"How..." was all she got out before she nodded.

"This just got a lot more complicated. What's his name and where can I find him?" Roman pulled his phone from his pocket.

"Why? What are you going to do to him?" Theodora asked wearily.

"Nothing at all. He's as safe as you are, and you're the safest person in the country right now. But he needs to hear this too."

Theodora didn't know what to make of his comment, but she wanted Sam with her. Deep down, she knew Roman wouldn't hurt them.

"His name is Samuel Matthews. He's wearing a black shirt and jeans. He's seated at the table next to the bar, close to the entrance."

"Good. I'll have someone bring him to us," Roman said as he texted.

Noticing her shaking, he took off his jacket and draped it over her shoulders.

"Thank you," Theodora sighed as she pushed her arms into the sleeves and pulling it close.

"Are you ready?"

She took a deep breath and nodded.

CHAPTER THREE

Lyzander could hear them talking in the corridor. All he could think about were her eyes.

They had held him captive the way his kind enthralled humans, and when she touched him, he couldn't pull away. With all his strength and gifts, he couldn't move. He simply stood there, shaking. He hadn't realised his body was even capable of doing such a thing. He'd almost crumpled to the ground when something had hit him in the chest. Something he was sure came from her. That human.

He was even more confused about what he had done.

He was always in control. In all the years he'd been alive, he had never lost control like that. He had never been so careless as to let a human see his fangs by accident. But when he saw Michael touching her, he simply reacted.

Hell, he knew he'd lost control as soon as he opened the office door. Even before he had stepped into the corridor, he could smell her. Her scent was unlike anything he had ever come across. Her scent made him endure extreme hunger, and not the hunger one of his kind would have after not feeding for three days. This hunger was so much more intense and overwhelming. There was only one reason why he hadn't tried to drink from her there and then.

He listened to her talk to Roman. When he heard the woman mention her husband, a strange feeling overcame him. One he didn't like and couldn't remember ever feeling before.

He threw back his glass of scotch and poured himself another, not that alcohol had much of an effect on him. He didn't know for sure what was happening. But from what he knew and what Roman had told the woman, he had a pretty good idea.

An idea he really didn't like, and certainly didn't have time for either.

The door opened but Lyzander didn't turn around.

"Take a seat. Can I get you a drink?"

"Yes please. Laphroaig, if you have it."

Roman raised an eyebrow at her choice and smiled. He went over to the bar where Lyzander stood, pouring four scotches. He knocked his back and handed one to Roman, just as a knock sounded at the door.

"Come in."

A large bald bouncer, built like a wall, opened the door halfway and leaned in.

"Hey Roman, you wanted me to bring this guy back here."

"Yeah, thanks. Show him in."

The bouncer opened the door fully and stepped out the way.

Sam went to Theodora. "Hey, baby. What's going on?" He kissed the crown of her head as she wrapped her arms around him. "Are you okay?"

"I am now,"

"Samuel Matthews." Roman offered his hand.

"Yes, and you are?"

"Roman Montgomery."

"Mr Montgomery. I didn't expect to meet you until Monday."

At this, Lyzander turned around and they both stared at Sam.

"Why would you be meeting with me?"

"I'm here to audit NocLife Leisure. The audit doesn't actually start until next week, but I thought we'd check the place out first."

"And the plot thickens," Roman muttered.

"If you didn't know who I was, then why am I here?" Sam turned to his wife. "What's going on, Teddy? Why are you in here? And what the hell is that on your neck?" Wide eyed, he reached out to touch her right side.

Theodora moved away subtly, pulling Romans jacket tighter around her.

"Teddy?" Lyzander spat the name out like it was

a poison in his mouth. "You're named after a child's toy?"

Theodora took offense, but it was Sam who answered.

"Teddy is a nickname. It's what I call her," he replied defensively.

"My name is Theodora."

"Ah, Theodora. Much better." Lyzander pronounced it firmly as he said her name for the first time.

"And who are you?" Sam asked with open hostility, as he took a good look at the pale intimidating figure peering back at him.

"This is Lyzander Pierce," Theodora explained to him.

"Ly... Ly... Mr Pierce? I'm sorry, I didn't know. I... Wait, what's going on here?"

"Please, have a seat, Samuel, and I'll try to explain what happened." Roman picked up the two other drinks, handing one to Theodora and offering the other to Sam. "Here, you're going to need this."

They took the drinks and sat down on the sofa Roman pointed towards.

"As much as I'd like to break this to you gently, it's already gone too far for the luxury of sugar coating. Now, where do I begin?" Roman pondered out loud as he stood in front of Lyzander. He looked at him, caught sight of something that made him smile and turned, giving Theodora his full attention as he spoke to the room.

"A few moments ago, Theodora," Roman suddenly paused, as though he had done something wrong, before hesitantly asking, "May I call you Theodora?" When she nodded, he resumed, "Theodora accidentally learned something about us. I would have said it was something she shouldn't have learned, but it would seem she was meant to know. As I watched the monitors earlier, looking out for trouble in the club, I saw the most confusing scene. A woman I'd never met before yet somehow I felt like I should know, fell out of the staff bathroom in a private area of the club. I watched as you stumbled into Michael, and he grabbed you by the throat and lifted you."

"Who did what?" Sam cried out but Roman carried on talking.

"I was about to go deal with the situation but Lyzander beat me to it. Unfortunately, in the process of helping you, he lost his temper and showed you more than he should have."

"You said us. Does that mean you're like him? Do you have fangs too?"

"Yes I am, and yes I do."

"Alright..." Theodora took a deep breath, sounding much calmer than she actually was, which made Roman smile. "Why are you telling me this?"

"Fangs? What the hell are you two talking about?" Sam asked, obviously frustrated and freaked out.

"The queue for the bathroom was long, so I came this way to look for another one. Some guy attacked me on the way out. But he wasn't just a man, was he?"

"No."

"What was he? What are you?" She asked Roman, but it was Lyzander who answered, looking only at her.

"He's a shapeshifter. Roman and I are vampires, and the reason he is telling you this is because you are a *keeper*. You are *my* keeper."

Theodora had no idea what he was talking about. But the way he'd said it and the intensity of his stare made her believe every word he said, and she didn't think it was a good thing at all.

"This isn't funny. I think it's time we went." Sam stated as he stood to leave, holding Teddy's hand. He looked back down when she didn't move and saw that she was staring intently at Lyzander.

"I assure you this is not a joke," Roman informed him.

"Come on, Teddy. Let's go." Sam tugged lightly at her arm.

"Theodora is not going anywhere." Lyzander stated harshly, but he seemed confused as he studied her.

"You can't stop us from leaving," Sam alleged, antagonizing the larger man.

"I saw his fangs, Sam, along with a whole bunch of other shit I can't explain. I think you should sit back down for a minute." Theodora tugged on his arm.

The movement pulled Lyzander's eyes away from her and he looked at the man holding her hand. That strange feeling he'd had earlier went through him once more, and he instinctively let his fangs drop down.

"You would be wise to listen to her," Lyzander rumbled. "I'm in the mood for blood." He couldn't hide the half smile that crept up at the sight of Sam turning pale and sitting back down.

"Lyzander!" Roman admonished for the second time that night.

Lyzander retracted his fangs but didn't stop glaring at Sam.

"I wouldn't normally say this as it's disrespectful and not my place, nevertheless, please excuse Lyzander this evening. He isn't usually like this. However, with his keeper in the room, he's understandably a little...touchy. So you, don't go provoking him if you want to keep your arms and legs attached to your body." Roman pointed at Sam who visibly swallowed.

"You really are va-vampires, aren't you? Sam stuttered.

"Yes."

"What do you want from us?"

"We don't want anything from you."

"What do you want from me?" Theodora spoke up then.

Roman looked over at Lyzander and the room fell silent.

Lyzander seemed to struggle for a moment before he gave a short sharp nod.

Roman turned back to them. "Vampires, among other supernatural creatures, are very real. We have worked and lived next to humans for a very long time. Despite what you may have read in your storybooks or seen in movies, not everything is true. Yes, we can be made by another vampire and those who were made into one of us were once human. Very special humans who were chosen specifically to be turned, as we can only turn those strong enough to survive the change."

"What if you make a mistake? What if they are not strong enough to survive? Does the person die?"

"No. They become what we call blood fiends. Dangerous, mindless abominations. It is against our laws to create them, and once we find them, they along with their creator are destroyed. Then, there are those vampires who are born."

"Vampires can have babies?" She blurted out in surprise.

Roman looked over at Lyzander, who gave a subtle shake of his head.

He didn't want Roman going into this right now.

It would only serve to freak her out even more.

"Yes and no. It's complicated and something we can discuss another time. Right now, this is what you need to know. Those of us who are born are what we call natural born vampires, and they are born with their soul. But at their first feeding, which for a vampire infant is blood, they lose their soul. When a human is made into a vampire and they take their first taste of human blood, the soul leaves their body, turning them fully from one of God's creation into a creature of darkness."

"But our souls are not lost. It attaches itself to the soul destined to be our other half. Our redemption. Our mate. It doesn't matter if that person is not yet born. That person's soul recognizes ours, and so becomes the guardian. The guardian may never meet the vampire whose soul they guard. However, once they do meet, they become bound to each other at first touch and the vampire will slowly regain his humanity. Guardian is an old term we never really use anymore. The name we use now is keeper."

Theodora inhaled loudly as she absorbed what Roman had just told them.

But just in case she had any doubts, Lyzander hammered it home. "You, Theodora, are my keeper."

Her face paled at his proclamation. "You must be mistaken."

"I assure you I am not."

"This is ridiculous. I'm not a keeper or guardian or whatever the hell it is."

"Deny it as much you like, but it won't change the fact that it has already started. I feel its presence already. We are now...bound." Lyzander spat the words out in distaste.

"Woah, back up there. What exactly has started?"

"And what exactly do you mean by bound?" Sam added.

Lyzander looked at Sam as though he were an annoying fly or petulant child. Turning his eyes back on Theodora, he inclined his head towards Roman who took his cue and carried on with the explanation.

"When you touched each other -"

"Why did you touch each other?" Sam asked almost accusingly.

"I was on the floor after that psycho shifter guy attacked me. Lyzander pulled me up."

"As I was saying, when you two touched, a connection was formed. And that connection will only get stronger. It can never be broken. You are now branded with Lyzander's mark." He motioned down the right side of her body.

Theodora didn't open the coat but she did allowed Sam to turn her head so that he could see part of the mark on her neck.

"It is the matching mark to Lyzander's. As a

keeper, your soul and the one you carry recognised him, linking the two of you together. From this moment on, you can never be parted and you must be joined in several ways if you are to survive."

"What?" Theodora and Sam exclaimed in unison.

Roman raised a hand to quiet them.

"You are not only the guardian of his soul but his soul mate. One cannot live without the other. In the beginning, it will be much harder. You must be close to each other, often, otherwise you will start to feel unwell. The longer you are apart, the worse you will feel, but only until you are fully bound. In the end, you must be bound. If not, it will result in a very painful and drawn out death. You must also share blood often. You are not entirely human, but you are not a vampire either."

"Then what the hell am I?"

"Supernatural. To stay healthy, you must have his blood and, to live, he must have yours. You must be intimate with each other."

"No fucking way," Sam shouted.

"This is not something I want either. I will be looking into a way around this," Lyzander stated flatly.

In spite of the crazy situation, his words were like a slap to Theodora.

"Then, there is the ritual –"

"Enough," Lyzander quietly warned Roman.

"I don't think so," Sam interrupted loudly, and the more he talked the louder he got. "You bring us in here with stories of vampires, blood and soul mates, but you only want to tell us half a story and expect us to eat all this crap up. I don't think –"

Before he could utter another word, Sam was across the room with his back against the wall and Lyzander's hand wrapped around his neck.

"No. You don't think, do you? Because if you did, you wouldn't be shouting at two, very old, and very powerful vampires. Even to an idiot like you, it must be obvious that I don't like you. I'm also in a very bad mood right now, so I would have no problem draining you dry and throwing your corpse in the bin, even though I'm sure your blood would taste like shit."

"Lyzander!" Roman admonished once again but Lyzander carried on.

"Let me be clear so there are no misunderstandings, Sam. Theodora may be married to you, but she now belongs to me. And since you seem to belong to her, that makes you both mine. Neither of you will be going anywhere," Lyzander hissed.

"Put. Him. Down!"

Lyzander's hand trembled as his head snapped around at the command.

He was stunned that this slight human woman was standing up to him. She looked pissed off and scared, yet strong and beautiful. As it registered in his brain that he thought her beautiful, he knew he was in trouble.

"And what if I don't?" He asked despite the slight tremble in his hand.

"You just said it yourself. You are both very powerful vampires. If you wanted us dead, you could have killed us before we even knew what was happening. But you haven't. Roman told me I can trust him, and I believe him. He also said that you would never hurt me. And you're right. Sam is mine and if you hurt him, that hurts me. And since you obviously need me for something, you won't do shit to him. So I suggest you put him down. Now!"

Smart girl, Lyzander thought, though he felt annoyingly compelled by her words.

"Fine. You may leave now." He dropped Sam to the ground and stormed out of the office.

He knew losing his temper in front of Theodora was the wrong thing to do, but he just couldn't think straight.

It was the thirst.

After three days of not wanting blood, he was suddenly ravenous. He blamed the thirst for his uncharacteristic lack of control and for why he'd listened to her instead of tearing Sam's head off.

* * * *

Theodora ran over and knelt down by Sam, embracing him tightly.

"Teddy, you saved my neck there, literally. But what the hell were you thinking. He could have really hurt you."

She shrugged. "I just saw red."

"That temper of yours is going to get us killed."

"My temper got us a reprieve, so let's get out of here before he changes his mind and comes back."

"He won't change his mind, Theodora. He's letting you go because he knows you will come back to him."

"The hell I will," Theodora rolled her eyes as they made their way to the door.

"You will know when to find him," Roman stated seriously, taking hold of the jacket she'd shrugged off and handed back to him. "Just don't wait too long."

Roman gave her the same look as he had in the hall, and she knew she needed to heed his words.

"Come on, Teddy, let's go." Sam pulled her out of the room.

Roman went back over to the monitors and watched as they made their way back through the club. His mobile vibrated in his pocket and he knew without looking that it was Lyzander.

"Have Josh follow them." He ordered without preamble. "If another supernatural so much as breathes in her direction, I want Josh to execute them. No exceptions. No one is to interfere with her, and that includes Josh. Only when she is ready is he permitted to reveal himself ."

"Got it. You know, Lyzander, she will be outstanding."

"No, my friend, she will be trouble."

* * * *

Lyzander prowled through the throngs of heaving bodies on the dance floor, looking for anyone who could quench his thirst, but no one stood out.

It had only been twenty minutes since Theodora and Sam had left but he could already feel his strength waning. Even though he was beyond hungry and the sound of beating hearts drummed out around him louder than the blaring music, he just couldn't find anyone he wanted to drink from.

Deciding to drink from one of the bags of blood he kept for emergencies instead, he turned to make his way back to the office. Just as he was leaving the dance floor, a soft feminine voice called out to him.

He turned and smiled down at the shapely, hazel eyed redhead before him.

She stood on tiptoes and leaned over to speak into his ear, her long and soft curls brushing against his cheek.

"I saw Roman earlier. He told me I might be of some assistance to you tonight."

"Ah, Gemma, impeccable timing as always. You

have no idea how good it is to see you right now."

Gemma beamed at his words as he waved her ahead of him towards the back office.

As a donor, Gemma knew who and what Lyzander was. Although she was fully human, she had friends in the supernatural world and often went to mixed events. It was at one of these events that she was introduced to Roman and Lyzander. They'd had a brief fling, which reignited if they saw each other when he came to town, and Gemma had been a casual blood donor to Lyzander ever since.

The office was empty when they entered and as Lyzander made his way over to the leather recliner, Gemma locked the door. She pulled her T-shirt over her head as she slowly made her way over to him and dropped to her knees, pushing his knees apart as she positioned herself between them. Gemma reached around to undo the clasp of her bra but Lyzander surprised her by stopping her.

"Not tonight, Gemma. I only require blood."

"But –"

"Only blood," He stated firmly, noting the confused look on her face.

He couldn't blame her for being confused. Not that it was necessary, but they usually fooled around a little when he fed from her. However, now he felt guilty just from having her in the same room as him.

"Okay, only blood. Where would you like to feed from?" Gemma asked salaciously as she started to undo the buttons on her jeans.

Lyzander's hand move to rest heavily on hers, stopping her.

"Your wrist will be fine, Gemma, and you can put your t- shirt back on too." She tried to hide the hurt that flashed across her face, but he saw it. "I appreciate you doing this. I have a lot going on right now so to do any more would be wrong," He explained, trying to placate her but got the feeling he had made things worse.

She smiled at him before putting her t shirt back on, offering him her wrist.

"It's fine. Whatever you need from me."

Her words and actions didn't match up.

Although she was smiling, he knew she was upset. As he held back curse, he thought, no matter the species he would never understand women.

* * * *

"What the hell was that?" Sam asked angrily as they hurried into their hotel room.

Not wanting to freak out the elderly taxi driver, they hadn't said a word the entire journey back.

"I don't know but that was some messed up shit. Maybe someone slipped us some acid or roofied us. Or maybe the sushi was bad or something. Anything that would explain a shared delusion."

"That was more than bad sushi."

"I know that. Don't you think I know that? My head is spinning here. Some guy claiming to be a vampire, who, by the way and just in case you missed it, is your new boss, says I have his soul inside me and that he owns me. Fucking owns me. Me! Like a pair of shoes he picked out to wear for dinner. I'm freaking out just a bit here, Sam. Just a bit!"

"I know, baby. I'm sorry, come here. I'm not mad at you. I'm just mad at the situation."

"What are we going to do?" Theodora whispered as he hugged her, pulling her over to sit on the bed.

"Well, right now, we're going to pack up and get the hell out of here."

"What about your job?"

"Fuck it. I care about you. Not working for some...thing that nearly killed me."

"But –"

"No. I'm a big shot auditor, remember? I can find another position somewhere else."

She smiled and squeezed his hand. "Thank you."

"No problem."

"What time is the next train?"

"That's what I was trying to tell you earlier. I think the first train back to Manchester is at 6am."

"Fuck! You know what? It's okay. We can have a couple of hours sleep, grab a taxi to the station and get the hell out of crazy town." Theodora groaned. "So we have a plan. God, I feel grubby as hell. I need to get out of these clothes. Why don't you rest up while I take a shower?"

"Sure, if that's what you want." Sam flopped back onto the bed and threw his arms over his head.

Theodora made her way into the bathroom, stripped off and stepped into the hottest shower she could endure.

She hadn't told Sam the truth.

She wasn't feeling grubby at all. In fact, she had been feeling colder and colder ever since they left the club, and now she couldn't stop shivering. She was also covering up a pain in her stomach that had been getting worse ever since she had touched Lyzander's hand.

After ten minutes of nearly burning her skin off, she felt a little better. As she reached out for a towel, she stumbled, hitting her shoulder on the shower door.

"Son of a..."

Theodora straightened up and wrapped the towel around her middle, feeling a tingling all down her right side. She wiped the condensation off the full length bathroom mirror with a hand towel and stared at herself in amazement.

She looked awful. Her face was tired and drained, but it was the tattoo that had her jaw falling to the floor. How she had missed it before she got into the shower only gave testament to how bad she was feeling.

The tattoo started just below her right ear, down

her neck, over her shoulder and arm, down the right side of her back and over her breast. It ran down her side over her hip and thigh, stopping just before her knee.

Thick black lines twirled and weaved their way down her body like vines. Smaller, more intricate lines and symbols mirrored the thicker lines. Some of them looked to be a language, but none Theodora had ever seen before.

It was beautiful. A work of art. A terrifying one at that.

Theodora vaguely remembered Roman mentioning a mark but she had never imagined anything like this. This wasn't a mark but a permanent branding.

Before she had time to freak out more, a wave of pain hit her and she crumpled to the floor. She took a few deep breaths and tried to pull herself back up, but another wave hit her and she cried out.

Sam burst through the bathroom door and stopped in his tracks.

"What the hell. Teddy, what's wrong?" He asked with wide eyes, crouching down to look at the tattoo.

Another wave of pain caused her to writhe around on the floor.

Sam pulled Theodora into his arms and carried her to the bed. "Tell me what's going on."

Theodora took a few deep breaths and the pain seemed to ease. She didn't answer him right away, choosing to keep the deep breathing going instead. She closed her eyes, concentrating on each breath. After a while, the pain eased even more and was almost gone.

She opened her eyes and looked up into her husband's worried face. "Pain, Sam. A really bad pain. I've...I haven't been feeling so hot since we left the club."

"And now?"

"A little better," she whispered.

"What about this?" He gestured to the tattoo.

"I know, and I don't know. I think I felt it happening though, when he touched me."

"What do you want to do now? If you're still in pain, we should go to a hospi–"

"And say what? That a possible vampire bond might be making me feel sick?" She shook her head firmly. "No, I just need to rest. The deep breathing helped so I'll just keep doing that for a while and get some sleep. I'll feel better once we're home." Sam shook his head and obviously wanted to say more but she added, "It's what I want, Sam. The pain has almost gone now anyway. I'll be fine."

Sam sighed. "Alright, let's get you under the covers before you catch a cold on top of everything else." He stripped off, climbed into bed and tucked them both in.

Within minutes, they were both sound asleep.

* * * *

Sam woke up to Theodora thrashing beside him, groaning in agony.

"Teddy!"

"Get..."

"What? What do you want me to do?"

"Get...me...back." She rasped out.

"There's no train for another two hours," Sam fretted.

Theodora shook her head. "Back to him. Now!" She managed to growl out through clenched teeth.

"Lyzander? You want me to take you back to him? The vampire?" He asked in amazement.

She nodded.

He hesitated only for a second before jumping out of bed, hurrying over to the suitcase to grab clothes.

Theodora cried out in pain. This wave was much stronger than any of the others. It felt like liquid fire was boiling her insides. She curled into a ball on her side with a whimper.

Sam tried to dress her but she wouldn't uncurl, her screams getting louder and louder by the minute. He was sure someone was going to call the police.

Theodora jerked at the sudden wave of pain and she knew she couldn't take any more. Everything went quiet in her head as she let out a soundless scream. Her vision began to blur. Sam's face etched in panic came into view, but it was the tall black man standing by the door behind him that caught her eye.

Then, her world went dark.

65

CHAPTER FOUR

Theodora inhaled deeply.

Coffee. Not the cheap instant stuff either, but expensive roasted beans that had been recently ground. It was odd she could tell the difference but it was a beautiful aroma to wake up to.

She took another deep breath.

There was something else there in the air too. Something rich, alluring, slightly piquant.

Sam must have made breakfast.

"What smells so good?" She murmured, placing her hand on a firm, bare chest.

"That would be me," came a deep voice. A voice that was most definitely not Sam's.

Her eyes snapped open just as a hand clamped down on her wrist and around her waist, and she looked up into Lyzander's sapphire eyes.

"Don't move away from me," he warned.

It was then that she realized they were lying together on a large Victorian, L-shaped brown leather, chesterfield sofa. She was wrapped around his body, with her arm and leg thrown over him.

Dressed in only a thin vest top and shorts, it felt far too intimate being wrapped around a stranger who was only dressed in lounge pants.

He must have seen the panic in her eyes as he warned her again. "Do. Not. Move." His expression was dark and his grip firm, though he wasn't hurting her.

"Tell me this is a dream."

"This is a dream."

"Really?"

"No," He replied haughty.

She wanted to curse at him but instead stayed quiet, taking in her surroundings.

They were in a living room, high up from what she could see of the city view through the wall to wall windows, which made up two of the larger walls.

"How did I get here?"

"Joshua, one of my men, brought you both back to me after you passed out."

"Where are we?"

"We're in one of the apartment buildings I own not too far from the club."

She glanced around.

It was a cosy room, with the lighting coming from several dim lamps dotted around. It was decorated in various shades of black, brown, grey, and white. There were a few paintings on the wall, one of which stood out the most.

It was a portrait of a man with long white hair and

blue eyes. For a moment, she had thought it was Lyzander but the plaque underneath it said 'Orsen'.

A large wooden unit in the room caught her eye next. It had quite a few books on it and what looked to be an entertainment center inside. The apartment was obviously a bachelor's pad but it still felt warm and welcoming.

"How long was I asleep?"

"Fourteen, nearly fifteen hours."

"What? Where's my husband?" Theodora tried to hide her fear, but something must have happened to Sam for him to stay away while she was unwell.

"Relax. He's resting in one of my guest rooms."

"What did you do to him? He wouldn't just leave me with you like this."

"He had no choice."

"What does that mean?"

"You were dying, and you needed me. I told him he could stay and watch you die or, leave and you would survive. I explained that if you died because he was too thick headed to listen to what was best, I would kill him. I gave him graphic details of all the ways in which I could slowly take his life."

Theodora's eyes widened in horror, but he continued before she could respond.

"I also promised you would come to no harm and would be feeling better by the time he saw you again. He's lucky I let him stay in the building. He really needs to learn his place," Lyzander muttered.

"His place is by my side. He's my husband. I want to see Sam." Quietly cursing, she went to move but Lyzander held her in place.

"I will only tell you one more time. Do not move! You almost waited too long to come to me. I won't let that happen again," he admonished as he rearranged her so that her body was still wrapped around his but they were now face to face.

When his hand accidentally brushed the side of her breast, she inhaled sharply, an involuntary reddening creeping up her neck and face at the intimate contact.

"Get off me, you freak. You can't just manhandle me like this," Annoyed at her body's reaction to a stranger, she wriggled, trying to get him to let go.

"Be still and keep quiet. If you listen to me, this will all go much faster. You need to hear what I have to say, woman. Then you may go and find your precious Sam," Lyzander practically spat the name out.

He hadn't meant to shout at her but he was hanging on by a thread. The damn woman was wriggling her body against him, and in no way did he want her to know the effect she had on him. She stopped struggling, and in return, he relaxed his hold but didn't let go completely. Despite his words, he failed to say anything for some time and simply stared at her.

Theodora's eyes locked onto his when she

noticed him openly studying her.

Her hair, her eyes, her ears and nose before finally lingering on her mouth.

Lyzander had been holding her for a little over fourteen hours straight now, and in that time, he had memorised every soft line, beautiful curve and adorable freckle that made up this woman, who was meant to be his mate. She was perfect, and Lyzander could already feel the tug-of-war going on inside him. She was a queen, and in another life, he would treat her as such, but he couldn't afford to let her get too close to him. As much as he could, he would have to keep her at bay.

Annoyed by his unabashed gawking, Theodora decided to take her fill of him too.

The first thing she noticed was his mark.

From what she had seen of hers and what she could see of his mark now, they matched perfectly down to the intricate vine-like patterns disappearing into his lounge pants. Looking at it up close, she realised just how beautiful it was but it scared her too. It was unlike anything she had ever seen before, and knowing that his mark now branded her skin was terrifying.

Some of his almost white blonde hair had been pulled back, leaving the rest to fall over his shoulders. It was thick and luscious, not a split end in sight. It looked like silk and almost seemed fake. His pale skin showed the odd line here and there, and she considered him to be in his thirties. Then she remembered that this man was in fact a vampire and could be much older.

He didn't seem as alabaster as he did when she first saw him, though he was still whiter than anyone she had ever come across. He had a long straight nose and a wide mouth with plump lips for a man. His symmetrical face was handsomely beautiful and her stomach gave an involuntary flip at the thought of being in the arms of this man like she was.

Lyzander had been watching her appraisal of him and his lips slowly parted. He let his fangs drop and waited for her reaction.

Theodora's heartbeat quickened and she gasped, her eyes snapping back to meet his.

"Do I scare you?"

"What do you think?" She replied defiantly.

The look on her face said that if she had the chance, she would stab him with the nearest pointy object she could get her hands on. But he knew better.

"I can smell your fear."

"And I can smell your breath."

Lyzander burst out laughing, shocking himself. It had been a long time since he'd laughed like that. This woman had backbone.

"That's right, I smell good to you," he replied cockily, taking in the slight blush that coloured her cheeks. "Don't be embarrassed. It is natural for us recognize each other in different ways, and scent is one of them. Do you want to know what you smell like to me, little keeper?"

"Not particularly, no, and it was the coffee I was referring to actually. The coffee smells good."

"Right." He drew the word out.

Lyzander retracted his fangs, unable to stop his half smile. He knew there was no way in hell he would let the bond be completed, but he couldn't help but like this fierce little keeper.

"Yes you scare me. I'm not stupid enough to not be scared of someone who could kill me. Doesn't mean I'm a pushover."

Lyzander was humbled, knowing such a strong human had been chosen as his intended.

"I don't think I'd like it if you were. I'm not your enemy, Theodora. I only want to help."

Her brows pulled together and her voice was almost a whisper when she spoke next. "What's happening to me?"

Lyzander grew somber. "You almost died tonight. The pain you felt was a result of us being separated. I felt it too, although I think I fared much better since my immortal body can take the pain. Your human one caused you to pass out. How do you feel now?"

"Better than I did before," Theodora grudgingly admitted.

"That's because we're together like this. With your skin touching mine, we are healing each other.

That is why I told you not to move. We started the bond when we first touched and my..." Lyzander took a moment as he struggled to say the words. "My soul. It wants to return to me. Until the bond is completed, we have to stay close to one another."

"This close?"

"At times, but not always. Being in the same room will be sufficient, most of the time."

"But this close when we are healing?"

"Correct."

Her mind and body were at war. She didn't know this man. It was unnerving how safe, how comfortable and right she felt in his arms.

She shook her head. "I can't be with you like this. I'm married. I don't want this bond."

"That's good, because neither do I. I'm going to be honest, Theodora, I have no intention of completing the bond with you. This is something that simply cannot happen. My world is violent and dangerous, and I need to be ruthless. I follow our laws. *I* am our lawmaker. I need to be feared. Getting my soul will only make me vulnerable and weak in a time when I need to be strong. We cannot complete this bond. But I cannot break it either. If we fulfill some of the steps, it should give us more time figure out a long term solution. We will still need to stay close but we won't be tripping over each other."

"Is this really happening?"

"Yes, and you need to understand everything that is happening and get on board with it, or we both die."

"Why?"

"Right now, we need each other to survive. If one dies, so does the other. We are irrevocably connected."

"Hold on a sec. Not that I knew vampires really existed before, but how can you die? I thought vampires were already dead, undead or whatever."

Lyzander rested her hand on his bare chest.

"Do I feel dead to you?"

She inhaled sharply. For a moment, she forgot herself as her hand lingered on his cool smooth skin, appreciating the form of his solid well defined pectoral, below which came the strong rhythm of a beating heart.

"No." She flushed, quickly taking her hand back.

"That is something all those stories about our kind keep getting wrong. I am very much alive. I was born this way not turned."

"So you're a natural born vampire? That's what Roman called it, right?" She continued at his nod. "Okay, so you were born a vam- Wait, vampires aren't immortal?"

Theodora's mind spun with all the questions she wanted to ask him.

"I can live forever. I will never age and my body will never decay. I am immortal, but death comes to us all, Theodora. I am well over one thousand years old. One of the oldest of my kind. There are only a few ways to kill me, and I am very, very difficult to kill. If the bond were completed, you would live as long as I. You would be as hard to kill as I am."

The idea of her being able to live forever was too much to deal with in that moment. She decided to push that thought to the back of her brain until she was finished freaking out over what she had learned so far.

"But this incomplete bond between us puts us in a dangerous position."

"Why?"

"I am old, Theodora. I have not lived this long without making enemies, and you have come into my life at a precarious time. We'll need to work out how to get through this, together. "

"Alright." Theodora sighed with relief.

The last thing she had expected was for this man, this vampire, to consider her side in this.

"As you have subtly mentioned many times, you are married." He raised an eyebrow and gave her a teasing look. "I'm not used to having contact with others, other than those donating blood to me. But you and I will need to be intimate, and often."

Theodora went to speak but he cut her off.

"Being intimate physically does not mean sex. I am suggesting..."

She noticed how uncomfortable Lyzander looked

as he trailed off.

He swallowed hard before continuing. "I'm suggesting touch, holding hands."

Had the situation not been so messed up, Theodora would have laughed at the uncomfortable look on his face. Instead of a powerful intimidating vampire, Lyzander was coming across like an awkward teenage boy talking to a girl.

"This is strange for me as it will be for those around me. My people are not accustomed to seeing things like this. It's very rare that I allow anyone the privilege of touching me, especially in public." He scoffed. "But we will need the physical contact to feel complete. If we are unwell or nervous, just a simple touch will do."

He knew that was something he would need to remind himself of constantly. He hardly ever touched others.

"I think I can handle that."

"Good. This thing, it's happening to *you* and *me,* Theodora. No one else can feel it. They can't grasp the full extent of what's happening and I have limited knowledge on the Keeper bond. I know it's been sometime since the last keeper was found and I certainly didn't think I would hear of another at this point."

"This is too important to mess up. I don't trust easily but I need to be able to trust you and you, in turn, have to trust me. We may not know each other but our souls do, and I can at least trust in that. I will never hurt you, Theodora. Believe me, I will always protect you with my life."

Theodora saw the sincerity of his words mirrored in the intense way he regarded her.

"Thank you, but I'm going to be optimistic. I choose to believe there will be no reason for you to put your life on the line for me. Neither of us want this bond so let's work together and figure a way out. We find someone who can break this bad boy, and then you can go find yourself a nice lady vampire and have some vampire babies. Sam and I will move far, far away and get on with our lives, and you'll live happily and literally forever after."

"That will never happen," Lyzander replied solemnly.

"You don't know that."

"I do. We are fated mates, you carry my soul within you. We can try to work around the bond, but it is not possible for it to be broken, only completed. If we are not together, then we will never be whole, which is fine by me as I do not want my soul. But you need to understand that there will never be anyone else for either of us."

"You forget that I'm already married."

Lyzander gave her a sad smile. She got the feeling he was pitying her.

"I will never have a vampire child, and you must resign yourself to the fact that you will not have children either. Neither of us will ever be able to have children with anyone else."

"What?"

"Vampires have only one chance at having children. Regaining our souls is what makes it possible for us to procreate. And the only person able to carry a natural born vampire child is our keeper. A vampire child is the only child your body will be able to carry. Should you ever try, no others would survive."

A tear escaped her right eye as she thought about her brief pregnancy.

If what Lyzander said was true, then her body was the reason their child hadn't survived. More tears came as she lay there, quietly thinking.

Lyzander used his thumb to wipe them away. "I'm sorry, Theodora."

"Why did you tell me that?" She whispered.

"Because you have a right to know."

"I'll trust you, Lyzander. For now."

"Thank you. We need to know each other to trust each other fully. So feel free to ask your questions, and I will ask mine."

"What else do we have to do to avoid pain and death and all things unpleasant?"

"Blood. We will need to exchange blood soon."

That sobered her up.

"I don't think I can do that."

"I'm sorry but you must if we're going to function

properly, especially while the bond is incomplete. Blood is what we need to keep each other alive."

"I need to talk to Sam about this."

"No." Lyzander stated firmly. "This is not for Sam, Roman or anyone else to decide. Blood is our fuel, our food. It gives us energy and heals us. I need to feed from you if I don't want to starve, and you need my blood in your system. Otherwise those pains will just continue, getting worse until you die of hunger too. The decisions we need to make from here on out are ours alone to make. I felt the pain too, Theodora. It was agony for me, so I know it must have been so much worse for you. We *need* to feed each other."

Theodora bit her lip. "Can't you just take blood from someone else?"

"I tried, and believe me, it did not go well."

"What do you mean? Did you hurt someone?"

"No, not exactly."

Theodora stared at him expectantly.

Lyzander sighed heavily before sitting up and twisting around towards her, moving her towards him while making sure their bodies were still touching at several points.

"I tried to feed after you left the club. I hadn't felt the need to in days. I should have been starved but I couldn't feed. Then I saw you and I was ravenous. So when Gemma, one of my donors, offered her blood, I forced myself to drink."

Theodora was surprised at the jealousy that flashed through her. It made no sense. Why would she be jealous? It's not like she wanted him to have her blood.

"Did you hurt her?" She asked with a little more grit in her tone.

"I already told you no. Though I may have hurt her feelings. I took her wrist and drank deeply, but on the second pull, I... the blood came back." He gestured with his hand in front of her then went quiet for a long time.

"I don't understand."

"It's never happened to me before, and I have never heard of it happening to my kind, ever. Vampires do not bring blood back up, but my body rejected it."

"You got sick?" Theodora stared. "You drank her blood then threw up on her?"

"Yes," Lyzander stated blandly.

"Gross," she muttered. "She must have been pissed."

"She wasn't pleased. I don't think she will be offering to donate again. Not to me anyway."

"Good."

Theodora's hand flew to her mouth. The word was past her lips before she had even realised it. Lyzander smirked but she carried on before he could comment.

"So you think you can only feed from me because

of this bond thing?"

"I don't think it. I know it."

"How?"

"I've fed from Gemma many times. Her blood normally smells pleasant, but this time, it didn't smell right." He scrunched his nose slightly. "It was...off. Old, dirty, like those trucks that collect rubbish."

"No wonder you threw up."

"But you, you smell delicious," Lyzander rumbled.

It was said with such frankness that she didn't want to reply.

Thankfully the ringing of his phone interrupted them.

Without taking his eyes off her, he reached across to the coffee table for it. He glanced down at the screen and seeing that it was Roman calling, he answered and put it on speaker.

"What is it?"

"Sorry to interrupt, but I thought you'd want to know Solomon Haywood just came into the club."

"Did he now?" Lyzander's eyes darkened.

"I take it he hasn't asked for permission to be in the area?"

Theodora's eyes widened.

"No, he didn't. And I don't think it's a coincidence that he's here either.

"Cleo and Chester are with him."

He hummed. "Really? Well, that is interesting

company for him to keep."

"Yes. Oh, wait...Gemma is with them too. She just sat down at their table."

"So much for never donating again." Lyzander sighed. "We'll be there soon. Keep an eye on them until we get there. Make sure those fools don't try to feed out in public."

"Will do." Roman said before Lyzander ended the call.

Theodora barely waited until the call ended to continue questioning him. "Why does this guy need to ask permission? Are you the leader of all the vampires or something?"

"Yes."

"So...the other two with this guy, are they vampires? Did they forget to ask too?"

"Yes."

"Do all vampires need to ask permission to come into your area?"

"They do if they want to live."

She swallowed loudly at his earnest explanation.

"I must know which vampires are in my vicinity at all times. Not all humans are good and trustworthy, are they? Well, it is the same for vampires. If, for example, there is a vampire known to cause trouble, I need to know why he is here. Has he come to cause *me* trouble? It's my job to make sure he doesn't go on a killing spree, exposing us all. We have laws which must be followed too. It is imperative that I know who is in my area, especially now. The timing of them showing up in my club is off."

"Why?"

Lyzander sighed. He hadn't wanted to get into all this yet but she deserved to know.

"Someone tried to kill my brothers. They came after me too, but whoever ordered the attack didn't know I was here."

"Someone is trying to kill you? Are you telling me I'm bonded to someone on a hit list? Oh god, you *are* going to get me killed." Theodora said, aghast and incredulous.

"No. My brothers and I make sure the rules are followed and laws are not broken in our world. I have power and control, which someone is obviously now after."

"Well, that's just great."

Lyzander recognized the generous dose of sarcasm in her tone and thought it best to put her at ease.

"You don't need to worry, Theodora. Whoever did this obviously has no idea who they are dealing with. But they will find out soon. I will see the terror in their dying eyes, and they will beg for a swift death as their blood spills in my hands when I tear their throats out. But enough of this talk. Come now, Theodora, it is time to feed." He cooed sweetly.

"Wow, you really need to work on how you

reassure someone. That little bit at the end there in no way eased my fears about you." She rolled her eyes.

"It should. You now know you are linked to someone who is powerful, merciless, and vengeful."

She groused, obviously agitated by the vampire.

"And it is how I must stay if I'm to keep us all safe. Now, let's feed. We can drink from each other's wrists. It won't be too much intimacy to begin with for either of us this way."

"I'm sorry but I don't think I can go through with it."

"You can and you will," he stated unflinchingly.

Theodora did not like his tone at all. No one bossed her around like that.

Obviously Lyzander was stronger than her, but she wouldn't let this vampire think she would simply do what he wanted. It wasn't in her nature. She always stood up for herself and what she believed to be right. She had to put up some sort of a fight even it ended up getting her killed.

"What if I won't?"

"Then I will make you."

Her eyes narrowed as she understood his meaning. "You wouldn't."

Lyzander leaned in close so their faces were almost touching. "I will pin you to the ground and force you to drink my blood."

Theodora gasped and, as much as she could,

shifted away. "You just said you'd protect me."

"And I will. Even from yourself. *You* are the one hurting the both of us if you refuse to drink my blood. So you will take from me, one way or another."

So much for considering her side in this.

"You ask me to trust you, then you threaten me. You're a monster."

"I am. But I'm a monster you *must* trust."

In a silent standoff, they stared daggers at each other.

"Take me back to Sam. Now," she demanded.

"After." He stated firmly.

A few more dirty looks were thrown before Theodora relented.

"Fine." She shouted, exasperated with the obnoxious vampire.

Lyzander gave her a cheesy self-satisfied smile that made her want to punch him in his smug face.

"Let's just get this over with. What do I need to do?"

"First, I will pierce my flesh for you since your teeth are dull. Then you will drink from me. I will then bite you and we'll drink from each other at the same time."

After a moment of repositioning their bodies in a way that made it easier to drink from each other, Lyzander let his fangs drop down and bit into his wrist. As sharp as they were, they pierced his skin as easily as hot knife gliding through butter.

Theodora watched as thick crimson blood erupted from two small puncture wounds in his pale flesh. The contrast was stark and unnerving, yet she couldn't pull her eyes away. As repulsed as she was at the idea of drinking blood, something inside her wanted this. She could feel it, willing her to drink. It was as if his blood was calling to her, for her.

Drink!

She took hold of his outstretched arm, lowered her mouth over Lyzander's free flowing blood and drank.

At the first taste of him, so many sensations hit her at once, setting off an explosion of flavors in her mouth and awareness throughout her body. She groaned her approval. It tasted metallic, but it was also sweet and warm. It was thicker than she had expected, but not like syrup.

Theodora gripped him tighter as she sucked harder on his wrist, groaning again. Her mind wanted to shut down at the thought of what she was doing. She was drinking blood, a vampire's blood. Lyzander's warm, delicious blood which she couldn't seem to get enough of now.

With every pull, she felt healthier, stronger, more aware of...everything. His blood made her feel full, though she hadn't known she was hungry, and whole though she hadn't felt incomplete. Drinking from him felt like coming home.

Lyzander didn't think she realized the noises she was making.

At her first pull, he had shuddered from the pleasure of it and sank back into the cushions behind him. The feeling was so good he had to take a moment to watch her.

He knew there was no way she would have hated his blood, after all they were intended mates. He was made for her. But it still pleased him to his core seeing how much she liked the taste of him. When a little of his blood escaped the corner of her mouth and she chased the drop with her tongue, licking his wrist before covering the holes again, a warmth rushed over him.

He couldn't wait any longer.

Taking one of her hands from around his own wrist, he raised it to his mouth and licked her wrist in return. Not because it would do anything but because after watching her chase his blood, he wanted a taste of her first before he got lost in the flavor of her blood. Then he bit down, his body jerking at the sensations that hit him as he drank her essence.

Her blood was pure. It was as though he was feeding on light, heat and energy all at once. It was powerful too, filling him up, giving strength to every cell in his body and making him whole. Suddenly, it was as though he could feel her within him and him within her. Desire overwhelmed him. Not only did his body now crave her, he also felt her yearning in return.

He lost track of time and everything around them. The more they drank, the stronger they became. It felt right and he knew she felt the same. The feeling was staggering, and his desire for her was becoming too much.

He was on the cusp of throwing her down on the sofa, pinning her down with his body and claiming her with a very primitive part of himself. But something within him pulled back. No, not something, it was her. As much at Theodora wanted him, she was confused.

She didn't want this.

She wanted Sam. She needed her husband.

That thought gave him the strength to pull away from her, unintentionally pushing her away from him in the process. Faster than the eye could see, Lyzander was across the room in front of the windows. Theodora had tumbled off the sofa, landing hard on her knees. Breathing hard and loud, she sat back and stared up at him.

He watched her, thinking about how close he'd come to losing control.

He had almost let that go too far.

No shit.

Lyzander heard the two words loud and clear in his head, as if they had been spoken aloud. But that wasn't possible. Was it?

Can you hear my thoughts, Theodora?

Theodora's eyes bugged out before she closed them. Standing, she turned away from him.

You can hear me, can't you?

He could feel the fear rolling off her. It wasn't from the bite. No, he had felt how much she had enjoyed it. He wasn't mistaken. She could hear him.

Can't you? Answer me!

She moved over to the sofa and sat down, facing away from him.

After a minute, when she still hadn't turned or said anything, he roared in his mind.

Answer me damn it!

She flinched then whispered, "Yes."

When she turned and looked up at him, her eyes were watery.

In that moment, Lyzander wanted nothing more than to hold her and give her comfort. The feeling was beyond alien to him. But it was the shock in her eyes that worried him.

"What?"

"You look..." She pointed at his hands.

Lyzander looked down and noticed his skin. The change was subtle but it was there. He looked across the room to see his reflection. To his surprise, he was no longer the near alabaster white he had been moments before. His skin now had colour to it. It was a slight difference but he looked more human.

"Shit." He looked at his hands again. If this

happened after one feeding, other vampires would soon notice. *This is not good!*

"Why can I hear you in my head?"

Lyzander was shaken by these new revelations. This wasn't supposed to happen, not yet anyway. He'd never intended for them to get close enough for any changes to happen at all.

"Sharing blood, it's brought us closer. Too close."

Only fully bonded mates were able to hear each other this way. He couldn't understand how this was possible after the first blood exchange. He knew he had to get away from her. He had to regroup, figure a way to keep her out of his head. He turned and walked away but stopped at the door.

"I'll send Sam up. I'll be back for you both later." Turning, he looked her dead in the eye. His face was less than friendly. "Do not touch him in front of me. If you do, I *will* kill him."

Overwhelmed with guilt and confusion, Theodora curled up into a ball on the sofa and let the tears fall freely when the door shut behind him.

* * * *

Theodora blinked sleepily. She must have cried herself to sleep.

Sitting up, she took another look at her surroundings and spotted her small travel case on the floor by the sofa. Suddenly feeling exposed in her pajamas, she hurried over to her case. Not sure how long she had before Lyzander came back, she put on the first thing she found, a pair of black jeans and a dark blue vest top. It was hard not to notice his mark down her right side so she dug around for her hooded sweat top, zipping it up just as the door opened and closed behind her.

"Teddy?"

Turning slowly, she saw Sam approaching slowly as though she were a wounded animal.

"Sam."

She threw her arms around him and he squeezed her tightly in return.

"I'm so sorry, baby. I had to leave you with him. He didn't give me a choice. Did he hurt you? Are you ok? How are you feeling?"

"I'm fine. He didn't hurt me." She sniffled.

Then she really thought about it.

She didn't feel fine at all. Her head was a mess but fine didn't describe how her body felt.

"Actually, I feel amazing. Incredible, invincible." She snort laughed. Then she found she couldn't stop laughing.

"What did he do to you?"

The worried look on Sam's face sobered her up and she stopped abruptly.

"He healed me."

"How?"

"He fed me his blood."

"What the fuck." Sam let go of her and ran his hands down his face.

"And he drank mine."

Sam started pacing the room.

"Oh my god, is he trying to turn you into one of them?" He exclaimed loudly as he came back to her, holding her again and inspecting her for obvious changes.

She shook her head. "No! No, it was his blood that healed me. The exchange of blood."

"Is this what he told you? Shit, has he brainwashed you already?" He sat them down on the sofa.

"Really, Sam? Do you really think anyone could brainwash me?" She asked the rhetorical question in a condescending tone, while at the same time giving him a look to let him know how stupid that idea was. Reaching down she pulled her converse trainers on. "He is not trying to turn me. He doesn't even want this bond, but we are both stuck, joined together. He's a dick but he is trying to keep me alive."

"How do you know he's not feeding you a line?"

Theodora took a deep breath as her eyes roamed the room, seemingly searching for an answer. But it wasn't the room she was searching, she was looking within herself.

"Because I can feel it, literally. The truth of what he said is in me. It's hard to explain, but having his blood did something to me. I know he's telling the truth but I also know there's something else. It's like I need to know something or I'm missing something so I have to trust my instincts. One thing I know without a doubt is that he will never physically harm me."

"Then why were you crying?" He wiped at her dry tear lines.

"When he took my blood...it felt... I'm so sorry. I couldn't help it." She reached for a cushion, holding it for comfort.

"Help what?"

"I was..." She dropped her head into the cushion and mumbled.

"What?"

Raising her head, she let out a big sigh and looked at the ceiling. "I said I was attracted to him...in that way. I'm sorry. I couldn't stop it. I love you, Sam, and I don't want him that way. Really, I don't. It's this stupid bond, and I know he doesn't want to want me that way either. I feel it, I felt it." Her eyes widened at how her last words came out. "Felt the way he was feeling that is, not anything else. Nothing else happened. I didn't mean-"

"Shhhhh, you're rambling. I get what you meant. Don't worry," he reassured her. Taking the cushion out of her hands, he pulled her into him for a hug. "You're going through a lot, Teddy, and I'm not gonna lie. I don't understand it or most of what's happening, but I'm here for you. You drank blood today. That's fucked up. No wonder you're a mess. But you're my wife, Teddy. You love me and that's all I need to know. I love you and, as I vowed on our wedding day, I'm yours for as long as you'll have me."

"Always Sam."

"Thank you for telling me everything. We've gotta stick together, keep each other strong. We'll find a way out of this mess together."

"Okay."

Theodora heard him even before he reached the door. So when it opened and Lyzander stepped in, she quickly moved away from Sam.

"I forgot to tell you one more thing. You can't touch me in front of him. Only when we're alone."

"You can't be serious."

"I am deadly serious. Don't touch her in front of me, in public or in front of anyone else for that matter. If you do, I *will* kill you. Test me at your peril."

Lyzander believed Sam was smart enough grasp that this was not something he should be tested on.

"Now, time to go. I have people to question." He motioned for them.

As Theodora went past and ahead of Sam, Lyzander warned,

Don't walk too close to him either. I won't hold back if he brushes against you.

She didn't look at him as she passed but he heard

her thoughts loud and clear.

Dick!

He had to fight back his smile as he closed the door.

It was the first time she'd voluntarily spoken into his mind.

CHAPTER FIVE

The journey was short and after Theodora had explained to Sam about the vampires in the bar, the rest of the drive had been silent, which she was grateful for. She'd needed the time to gather her thoughts.

They entered the Veil early enough, and even though the club didn't usually get going for another couple of hours, the bar always attracted a few pre-drinkers because of its location. The music was playing a little lower at this time of night and Theodora was surprised to see several booths were already busy with what looked like several exclusive private parties.

Glancing at one booth, she watched as the revelers downed a round of shots. She thought it a little early for shots, they weren't going to last long. Then again, maybe a shot was exactly what she needed.

Lyzander abruptly turned, making a beeline towards a bar on her right and the bartender promptly made his way over.

"Mr Pierce. What can I get for you?"

"A shot of bourbon for the lady please, thanks Mike." Remembering Sam was now with them, he said, "make that two."

Theodora gave him a side-eyed glance of disapproval.

Stay out of my head!

It's not something I can help doing. He watched Roman approach. *Besides, I ordered what you wanted, so don't be ungrateful.*

Theodora's side-eye morphed into a full on glare.

Oh, I'm grateful for the drink but I'd be more grateful if you didn't speak to me in my head.

She turned and Roman came to a stop in front of her. With a subtle bend of his head, he nodded in her direction.

Regina

She heard the words clearly, but for some reason, it sounded different.

You're the one who started this conversation. It would be rude of me not to answer.

Lyzander smirked when he heard Theodora's replying growl.

What does Regina mean anyway?

Roman's eyes widened in surprise.

You heard that?

"No! No! No! Not you too." She groaned aloud.

"What's wrong?" Sam looked between her and Roman.

She can hear me!

Yet another shocking revelation for Lyzander to deal with. But with other vampires in the bar, especially the three intruders in his territory, he had to be careful.

We can't discuss this here, Theodora. If you can hear and speak with both Roman and I, who knows if the other vampires can communicate with you too.

Theodora followed the direction of his gaze.

"What's wrong?" Sam asked again, oblivious to the silent conversations.

"So, so much. I'm not even sure where to begin."

Just then, Theodora caught the thoughts of someone else on the other side of the room.

There he is.

The thought came from a woman who was staring intently at Lyzander. This woman was one of the vampires he'd come to see.

"Now is definitely not the right time to talk about this, Sam."

She looked over again to a table where two women and two men were sat, watching them.

Sam followed the direction she was looking in. "Alright but we will talk, later."

Is that them? The vampires who didn't ask for permission?

Lyzander nodded in reply.

"Roman, would you mind keeping Sam company while I greet our uninvited guests?"

"Of course."

"What if I prefer to wait alone?"

"No!" Both Lyzander and Theodora stated.

Realizing there could be other vampires in the room, she got the feeling it was safer if he wasn't alone but Sam did not look happy.

"Come, Theodora."

She smiled by way of an apology at Sam as Lyzander lead her away. She could tell he wanted to say a lot more and was grateful he didn't. She couldn't blame him for being upset though, he was already putting up with a hell of a lot for her.

"Come on, Sam, let's get you another drink," Roman prompted. "I have a feeling you'll need it."

* * * *

Roman took him to an outdoor balcony garden just beyond the **VIP** area he and Theodora had joked about when they'd first arrived at the club. Roman placed a drink on the table and sat facing him.

Sam pushed the drink away. "I'm really starting to hate that guy."

"I can tell. This is a lot to take in."

"No shit."

"I must say you're handling all this remarkably well so far."

"Like I have a choice."

"No, you don't."

"I should be down there, not him. I'm her husband, I should be the one protecting her."

"From the three very old vampires? I don't see how you'd manage that. No, Lyzander will protect her. She is his soul keeper and fated mate, which means they have belonged to each other since well before you were born. Forgive me if I'm wrong, but I do believe a soulmate trumps a husband. "

"And here I was thinking he was the asshole."

"He is. I'm not being mean, Samuel. I'm being honest with you. He doesn't desire her as you do, and he cannot have her as a mate if he is to keep us all alive."

"So let me get this straight. He *really* doesn't want her? If that's the case, why not just leave us alone?"

"Because that doesn't mean he can stop the pull towards her. This bond makes him need her and he's never really needed anything in his life. He won't ever let her go, but he won't let anyone near her again without his permission either. That includes you. It's our primal nature as vampires to protect what is ours and unfortunately, Lyzander can be more primal than the rest of us. He may not want her but he has most definitely claimed her as his. Their bond has begun to form and it's strong. You need to accept that there's no going back."

"Is that supposed to make me feel better?"

"Yes it is. I'm trying to explain things so you understand that she is safe."

"Okay, I get it. No one is going to touch her. But where does that leave me?"

"It leaves you here with me. Don't worry, Samuel, I'm going to keep you safe. I won't let any harm come to you."

Sam eyed Roman wearily. "How do I know you're not going to eat me?"

Roman let out a hearty laugh. "Because I don't eat my employees."

"What?"

"That would be bad for business, though I will take a sip if offered." Roman teased.

"I don't understand."

"NocLife, Sam. You said it yourself when we met that you were due to start on Monday. As of now, you work for me. I called your office and spoke to Mr Prichard. I explained that you are now *permanently* a part of the NocLife family, exclusively. I've claimed you as mine."

"What? How? No! I'm not gay."

Roman laughed. "I know that, and neither am I. This is not a bond, but a claim and a vampire claim is protection from all other supernaturals. I told you before, we protect what is ours, and you, Samuel, are now mine."

"Other supernaturals?" Sam groaned. "This is too much, I can't handle any more."

"But you must. Theodora needs you to. This is just the beginning. Something is coming and I'm betting it's a shit storm of trouble. Lyzander needs to be strong, which means she does too, and when it gets really bad, she is going to need someone to lean on. That someone has to be you. So suck it up for all our sakes."

"Shit!"

Sam reached across the table and grabbed the tumbler. Sniffing the glass, he recognized the whiskey and took a big swig.

"Other supernaturals? How many others are there?" Before Roman could speak, Sam cut him off. "You know what? I don't want to know. Let's keep that on a need to know basis and I don't think I need to know right now." He added before knocking back the last of his whiskey.

"As you wish."

"Tell me about this protection claim. How does it work?"

"When a vampire claims a human, all other supernatural can smell the vampire in their blood. That's how they know the human is protected."

"What do you mean by smell the vampire in their blood?"

"The human must willingly accept and ingest at least one drop of the vampire's blood for the claiming to take."

Sam eyed Roman silently for a moment as his mind added things up. "You said you had claimed me!"

"Yes."

"That's not possible. That's something I'd remember." He said, panicked.

"It's done."

"When the fuck did I willingly drink your blood?"

Roman looked down at the empty tumbler in Sam's hand.

Sam's eyes followed.

"Son of a-"

Sam launched the glass but Roman was across the room, leaning against the door before the glass could shatter at where he'd been sitting.

"You need to know that I would give up my life for Theodora, so I can't risk her doing something stupid to protect you. Sorry, Sam. I actually like you. That's why I volunteered to claim and protect you. It was a shitty thing to trick you like that, but I knew there was no other way you would accept my blood."

Roman decided to give him a few minutes alone to calm down.

Halfway out the door, he turned back to Sam. "Welcome to our world, Sam. Trust no one."

And then, he was gone.

* * * *

As they walked towards the booth where the vampires were, Theodora caught another errant thought from the woman.

One touch

She didn't know what it meant but she could feel the desperation coming from the woman. Desperation was pouring off all three of them but it felt different with one of the men. With the other two, it was a malevolent vibe but he was more anxious. He needed something from Lyzander.

She wasn't sure how or why she knew all this, but since drinking Lyzander's blood, she felt more attuned to everything and everyone. On one level, she knew she should be terrified but something about it came all too naturally for her to feel real fear. She pushed that thought to the back of her mind for the time being.

She was so focused on trying to hear more she hadn't noticed they had reached the booth where the three vampires had come out of and were now standing in wait while one of the women sat watching. She figured the woman had to be Gemma, Lyzander's donor.

"Cleo, Chester, Gemma." Lyzander said their names in greeting, and they lowered their heads in return. "Is Ora not with you?"

"No, not this time. Ora said she had errands to run, whatever that means." Chester mumbled the last part.

Ora and Cleo, the hot and sultry twin daughters of a southern preacher, were turned vampires. Their maker, Atticus Forbes, took a liking to them and wanted to keep them for himself. Only, he couldn't quite control the feisty pair as they were a law unto themselves once he had turned them. So he decided to go back to their family home and turn their older brother, Chester, making him their custodian. Unfortunately, Atticus was killed by another vampire in a dispute a year later.

"Are they still giving you the run around, Chester?"

"Ugh, you have no idea," he replied sounding defeated, running a meaty hand down his face.

Lyzander shook his head. He really needed to grow some balls.

"Lyzander, you are looking well. Your establishment is, *charming* as always."

Theodora didn't think he meant it at all.

"Solomon Haywood, has your time finally come?"

Solomon, tall and thin with pale skin and long back hair down to his shoulders, tilted his head in question.

"I assume you wish to end your immortal life and have come to me for death. You must want me to put you out of your misery. I mean, why else would you show up in my territory without permission, unless you wished for death.

"My apologies, but there was no time to get permission."

"They have these things now, Soloman, they're called phones. You pick one up, dial a number to make a call and instantly, you can talk the person on the other end of that call." Lyzander drawled sarcastically.

"You know I don't own one of those things."

"I forgot, you prefer the prehistoric days."

"I hate technology."

"Because you are stubborn and snobbish and refuse to learn."

"I learn. I just prefer the old ways."

"Pictographs?"

"Pen and paper, Lyzander. People don't send letters anymore."

"They do, just not to you. You could have had someone call for you but you chose to come to me this way. Why are you here?"

"I am here regarding my progeny."

"Noah?"

"That impetuous boy will be the death of me."

"Yes, you may be right, unless you have a good enough explanation."

Solomon only smiled at this. He didn't seem worried. "I do, but it is a delicate matter."

He obviously didn't want to talk in public. But before he could continue further, the female vampire interrupted.

"My, my, Lyzander. There's somethin' different bout you." Cleo, a tall curvy woman with long wavy candy red hair, played with a lock as she took a step closer to him.

"Really?"

"Don't get me wrong, you still look good enough to eat." Cleo licked her lips and surveyed Lyzander's body salaciously before finally finding his face again. "But you seem...different."

Just a little closer.

Theodora watched the woman wearily.

Cleo was truly stunning and there had obviously been something between her and Lyzander. As much as she hated to admit it, those two things alone made her feel a pang of jealousy. But they weren't the sole reasons she felt that something was off about this woman.

On some deep down level, she knew she should be afraid of this beautiful vampire, but she wasn't. Something was going on, and it had her fight or flight kicking in instinctively. Theodora felt something root her to the spot and she knew without a doubt this wasn't a day for running.

"I'm the same cold bastard I've always been."

Cleo laughed playfully at Lyzander's comment.

Just one touch.

"I see you're still tightly wound. Maybe you need help with that, relievin' all that stress you been holdin' onto." Cleo dropped the lock of hair she had been twirling and reached over to lay a hand on Lyzander's chest.

It was as though time had slowed for Theodora.

He'll never know what hit him.

"Stop!"

Theodora's words were loud and clear.

Lyzander noticed Cleo's eyes widen in surprise before she dropped her hand.

"Well, well, well. What do we have here" Cleo inhaled deeply.

What's wrong?

Lyzander could sense the tension rising within Theodora.

I'm not sure, but something is up. You can't trust her. I just feel it.

Lyzander felt the urgency as her thoughts came and she moved closer to him.

"Seems you' been replaced Gemma, and it looks like his new blood bag is the jealous kind. Real pretty though, no wonder he got rid of you." She laughed.

Theodora felt bad for the girl. She had gone red either through anger or embarrassment.

Cleo turned back and looked right at Theodora. With a smile, she reached over and tried to touch Lyzander once more.

"I said stop." Theodora didn't raise her voice but the authority in her tone came through.

Cleo frowned as she realised she was unable to reach forward.

"Don't touch him. Don't touch anyone in Lyzander's club. In fact you need to leave, now." Theodora didn't know where this was coming from, but she felt it in her core that what she was saying was right.

"You' gonna make me, precious?" Cleo goaded.

You need to get her away from here, Lyzander. She's poison, or poisonous, or something. I don't understand but she needs to go. Now!

"Leave." Lyzander ordered sternly.

"What?" Cleo was taken aback.

"Leave now. If you are still within my area at sunrise, you will be put to death."

"You'd cast me out just like that?" Cleo exclaimed, livid.

"Yes."

"Bitch." Cleo moved as if to take a step in her direction.

Theodora moved back on instinct and as she did, one side of her hooded top slipped, revealing part of the mark she now shared with Lyzander.

The three vampires inhaled sharply, but it was only Solomon who bowed his head at her.

Regina.

"Time to leave, Cleo." Chester bowed and grabbed hold of his sister, pulling at her arm. Turning back to the booth, he called to the girl watching them. "You comin', Gemma?"

Gemma looked longingly at Lyzander before shooting Theodora a look of disdain. Knowing there was no reason for her to stay, she stood up and made her way over to Chester's side.

Lyzander watched as Cleo stared daggers at them

as she was dragged away by her brother. He turned back to the remaining vampire before him.

"Come, Solomon. Let's talk in my office. Maybe you can give me a reason not to kill you."

CHAPTER SIX

Theodora and Solomon were seated at Lyzander's desk across from each other. Lyzander stood behind her, to her right, with his hand resting on the back of the chair. They looked like a royal portrait come to life.

"Congratulations," Solomon said, breaking the ice. Bowing his head first at Lyzander and then Theodora. He looked at her with a mixture of longing, sadness and awe. "It has been a long time since the last awakening."

"Too long," Lyzander solemnly replied.

"It is my honor to meet you." He bowed his head deeply to Theodora.

It was said with such reverence she wasn't sure what she was supposed to say in return.

"Uh, you're welcome?" It was less of an affirmation and more a question.

When he raised his head, he had an easy smile for her and she sensed his approval.

"Why are you here?" Lyzander was tired of the pleasantries.

"I've heard rumors that someone has been trying to recruit vampires who are known outsiders, those who normally keep to themselves, those with certain qualities."

"Like Noah?"

"Exactly. I'd decided to go to ground a few days ago, but within hours of being at rest, Noah came to me." Solomon gestured to his head, meaning they spoke mind to mind. "He told me he had been approached by a group who wanted him to join in the fight against the current régime. Wage a war to wipe out the council and the old weak ways, to take back power and rule over the humans, and treat them as the cattle they are. These were their words, not his. He warned me not to trust anyone as someone high up must be involved, going by the information they already had. They told him to pick a side."

"And did he?"

"He told them he'd picked his side a long time ago when he chose to be turned by me. They didn't like that and warned him he was on dangerous ground. That he had two choices and there was no room for indecision. He was either with them or against them. He explained that my side is where he was born into this life, and it's where he would die when the time came. They tried to force the issue and he had to kill most of them in return. Fools. Anyway, he said to me if there is going to be a war, he wants to fight with me. I arose shortly after planning to go to him. Only, I awoke to the news that the Council had been attacked."

"So it's common knowledge now?"

"Not yet. I only know because I have my fingers in many pies."

"And lots of spies everywhere."

"You don't get to live as long as I have without information."

"Yes, and there are only a handful of you left from my father's generation."

"My god, that makes me sound old."

"You are old and powerful too. I suspect you may even have power to rival my own. With everything you've just said, it's interesting that you arrived with such dubious company. So I'll ask you again, Soloman, why are you here?"

"Cleo and Chester arrived at my home just before I set out. They wanted to talk to me, to persuade me that I should be on the right side of the fight to come. I'm not sure who's running things, but Cleo and Chester are definitely with them. I told them I'd already heard about the council attack and that I was coming to retrieve my progeny. I didn't mention I was on my way to see you. They couldn't sense any lies from me because what I gave them was the truth. But *I* could sense all the lies coming from them when they told me they were coming here to talk to you."

"I could have easily ripped their hearts out, and watched them disintegrate in front of me before either of them knew what was happening. But even with all my informants, I still don't know who is watching and waiting to make their next move. So until he is with me again, I won't risk Noah's safety that way. The reason I came here..." Solomon stood up, pushing his chair back in the same movement. "Is to pledge my allegiance to you." He threw his right arm across his chest, his fist closed, resting above his heart. "My king."

Solomon looked over at Theodora. "My queen. I am yours, from this moment to my last, when to the dust I shall then return."

He dropped to one knee and bowed. "Meus rex. Regina meis."

A surge of power flowed through them.

Theodora managed to stay silent as she tried to take everything in.

Lyzander was stunned.

Although he was rightfully king by birth, he had never claimed the title. He'd always governed with his brothers who made up the council, and vampires had always followed their laws. But he'd never before asked anyone to take the kings oath. Roman had taken it the day he was turned but they were more like brothers.

The oath wasn't a small matter. The only way for one to be released from it was death. For one as old as Soloman, to offer it was astounding. It worked in a similar way to the wolves and their alpha. Lyzander would have control over Solomon as his leader and in doing so, some of his power was transferred to them.

"Rise, Solomon."

The men stared at each other for long moments.

"You did not have to do that." Lyzander finally broke the silence.

"I wanted to. It felt like the right thing to do."

"I never would have asked you to do that."

"And that is why I did it."

"Thank you."

"You are most welcome, my king. If you don't mind, I do have a small request. I'm here to stand and fight for you but-"

"Noah," Lyzander interrupted, already sensing Solomon's emotions and his urgent need to find his progeny.

"Yes."

"Go, get him. I'll arrange a place for you to rest when you get back."

"Thank you. I should only be gone an hour or two."

"If you need anything, just let Roman know and he'll arrange it for you. We'll talk again tomorrow."

Solomon smiled at them before turning to leave the office.

Lyzander pulled a chair over from the monitors

and set it beside Theodora, turning her so they were facing each other.

"Did you feel that?"

"Yes. When Solomon pledged the oath, he submitted to me. To us. And by doing so, he shared some of his power and strength with us."

"Right." She dragged the word out. "And Regina? I've been called that name by almost everyone I've met. I've put together a few things from what Solomon said, but I need to hear it from you. What does it mean?"

Lyzander met her gaze. "It means queen. You are their Queen."

"I can't take this." She stood up abruptly and paced the room. "It's too much. One minute I'm having a fun weekend away with my husband and the next, I'm the queen of real life vampires! I think I'm losing my mind. Maybe I've already lost it. That's it, I've gone bat shit crazy and I'm locked up in a padded cell somewhere. All of this is just in my head." She babbled.

"It's not in your head. This is real Theodora and you know it. You feel it. I know it's a lot to take in, I get that, but I need you to stay with me."

"How can you get it?" Her voice grew louder as she spoke. "There's no way you get this. You're a vampire, you're part of my problem. You're not meant to be real, you're a freaking supernatural being."

"I hate to break it to you, love, but so are you. Keepers are supernatural too. Regular humans generally don't look after the souls of vampires or hear the thoughts of others."

"Regular humans? Oh god, I'm not even human anymore, am I? I'm a damn keeper. I'm a freak. I'm a–"

"Queen."

She didn't even see him get up from the chair. The feel of his skin against hers was calming as he held her close, touching her hand. It was soothing yet frustrating for them both.

"You are our queen, and you can handle this because you are strong. You wouldn't be here if you weren't strong enough. You were destined not just to be a keeper, but my keeper. *My* queen. You know I'm speaking the truth because you can feel it."

He took a step back, releasing a sigh and her at the same time.

"And I do get it, Theodora. Yesterday I was part of a government, which I ran alongside my brothers. We looked after my world and made good and fair decisions together. Today, I am a king, who has a queen, who has a consort. I'm in half a bond which I cannot complete, a bond which puts us all in danger. And now, I have to make major decisions without my brothers' council for the first time in hundreds of years. And if that wasn't bad enough, we seem to be going to war too. So if you're feeling overwhelmed,

Theodora, I get it."

He looked down at her, and the tiny gap between them felt like a canyon. Reaching over, he took a handful of her hair and idly played with it.

"Well, damn. I didn't think you'd get so worked up about it."

"I don't get worked up."

Lyzander hadn't raised his voice. He seemed calm on the outside, but with their new connection, she could tell he was freaked out and his rising panic seem to be calming her own.

"You just got all ranty."

"No, I did not."

"You did. I know a rant when I hear one. I'm the queen of emotional rants."

"You are the queen of vampires. Yes, it's a lot to take in, but only for your mind. We are only just getting into this but it feels right."

He dropped her hair to rest his hand over her heart.

"It feels right here, doesn't it?"

"Yes," she grudgingly whispered.

"Then you have to hold it together. Your mind will catch up to what your heart already knows. We're virtual strangers, but you know me in here. You know who you really are and recognize what you're meant to do." He tapped two fingers above her heart. "But not here. Not yet." He tapped her temple before resuming playing with her hair again.

"Trust your instinct. It will keep us alive."

Lyzander pulled her close.

She didn't recoil, but instead sank into the temporary comfort he was offering.

Sensing her confusion, he reached along their bond. She longed for his touch, yet loathed it at the same time. This was something he understood well.

Lyzander buried his nose in her hair, inhaling deeply. The sense of relief it brought him was disturbing. They had only known each other for less than forty eight hours, and already, the connection between them was strong. He had to remind himself that theirs was a bond that could never be completed.

Releasing her, he went over to the bar and poured two fingers of whiskey.

"Speaking of instincts, what was that with Cleo?"

Taking the tumbler, she knocked it back and handed him the glass. She worried her lip, struggling with the need to be close to him. Deciding she needed space, she leaned against the door, facing him.

"I could hear her, but not the way I hear you and Roman. I heard her thoughts. She was desperate to touch you, and no, not in a sexual way. It was more like she wanted to do it before she was caught. I don't know what her plan was but I think she was trying to poison you."

Lyzander seemed surprise as he knocked back his

own drink.

"You heard this?"

"I heard her thinking "one touch would be enough", but it wasn't just what I heard. It was what I felt. I got a bad vibe from her." She shrugged. "Maybe it was my instinct kicking in."

"Maybe. When you told her to stop, she did."

"Yeah, I'm sorry about that. I don't know what came over me, but I knew I could make her stop. I wasn't afraid. I had to make her listen."

"You did. As vampires, we are able to control humans with a little mind manipulation. What we don't have, is the ability to control those of our own race. You are neither vampire nor human. You made her stop but you shouldn't have been able to do that. We've only had one feeding. How can you be so strong already? But I think I could feel your power even before that."

He said the last part more to himself and Theodora could sense his worry.

"What does that mean?"

"Honestly, I've no idea."

She had more questions but he raised a hand to stop her.

"Roman is here. He'll take you to Samuel. You need your husband right now, and frankly, I need some space too. This closeness, it's too much. Go talk to Sam and clear your head. I'll find you soon."

Theodora straightened up off the door just as

Roman opened it.

"Thank you."

She took one last look at Lyzander before following Roman out into the hallway.

Lyzander let out a sigh as soon as the door clicked shut.

He thought things were bad before, but finding out Theodora might be able to control vampires was a disaster. Their bond was incomplete and had to remain so, which left them both vulnerable. If vampires, especially the ones waging the war found out she had the ability to manipulate them the way they did humans, she'd become a walking target. No vampire would be happy with that.

He was already feeling anxious and she'd only just left the room.

He hated this damn bond with a passion.

CHAPTER SEVEN

It was still fairly quiet in the main area, though there were one or two booths taken up by private parties.

Roman had taken Theodora up to another level of the club. She had barely taken in the VIP area when he steered her to a private garden balcony which overlooked the city. Roman said something about giving them privacy and getting some food for her, but she didn't take much notice of anything else he said as he'd left her at the door.

Seated at the far side of the balcony, Sam caught her attention. He looked deep in thought as he stared off into the night sky.

She made her way over and sat down beside him. "Hey." She gently bumped his shoulder.

"Hey."

"How you doin'?"

"I'm good."

Theodora gave him a knowing look.

"I'm good. Okay, maybe not so good. I'm confused, I'm annoyed and I'm pissed the hell off after Roman roofied me with his blood. He officially claimed me as his, all apparently for my own protection. Then he went off to go get me a sandwich like it was no big deal. I can't do a damn thing about anything that's happening in my life right now, so I'm out here quietly freaking the fuck out. But other than all of that, I'm good."

"Blood roofie?"

"Uh huh."

"Well, shit."

"Yeah shit. So what happened out there?"

Theodora took a deep, audible breath before answering.

"Well, I'm pretty sure I just met two of Lyzander's exes. One was a human blood donor, who he had cast aside because of me. She hates my guts and wishes me nothing but pain and misery. We didn't speak, but I could tell by the hate-filled glares and hostile vibes she sent my way. The other woman was a vampire who was trying poison him, but I managed to foil her plans. So now she also hates me, yay!"

"Aside from the whole being mated to a vampire madness, Lyzander turns out to be the king of all vampires, which makes me the queen of freaking vampires! I know this because someone just pledged fealty to me, their queen! That was weird."

"I also have this strange telepathy shit going on which I can't control. I can't seem to be able to keep

Lyzander out of my head or stop myself from hearing other vampires' thoughts either. Oh, and I almost forgot, I possibly have some odd power that is freaking the hell out of Lyzander. Which isn't actually a good thing. So yeah, I'm good too." Theodora spoke quickly in that rambling way she only did when nervous.

"Wow, what a pair we make."

"The next time you suggest a weekend away, I'm choosing where we go!"

"Absolutely. This whole thing sucks. Pardon the pun."

"You're right. It sucks." She sighed. "What are we going to do, Sam?" She was much calmer now that she got that all off her chest.

"Honestly Teddy, I don't know. It's happening too quickly for either of us to digest. I'm a numbers guy, you know that. I like my facts and figures. I like to read and research and have as much information as I can before making a decision. This is not supposed to be real. It's fantasy. This is one big game to those vampires. You and I have been dragged into a world that we didn't even know existed two days ago. We're now players in a game we know nothing about. We need to figure out the rules so neither of us are blindsided again."

"But how do we do that?"

Sam took a moment to gather his thoughts.

"Roman, he reminded me that I now work for

him. I'm going to find out as much as I can from him and anywhere else I'm given access to. You find out what you can from Lyzander and we'll pool whatever info we find out. It's a weak plan, but I'm tired and hungry and I can't think straight, so it's all I've got right now."

"It's good, Sam. It's better than what I've got anyway."

"Thanks. We can do this, together." He bumped her shoulder.

Theodora rested her head on his shoulder for comfort. She only got to enjoy their closeness for a moment before he moved away.

"First things first, I need to find a bathroom pronto and then I need to eat something. Roman better go all out on that sandwich. I'm bloody starving. You must be too. It's been a while since either of us ate anything."

Theodora wasn't starving at all. Drinking Lyzander's blood had filled her up and given her the nourishment her body needed. But she wasn't going to explain that to Sam.

"I could eat."

"I'll be right back." Sam stood and made his way over to the door. "Are you going to be alright?"

"Yeah, I'll be fine. I'm the badass queen of vampires, remember."

Sam gave her a sad smile before pushing open the door. "Back in a minute. We'll talk this plan over some more then. Don't worry."

And then Theodora was alone.

She looked out into the inky night sky, contemplating not only what Sam had said and what Lyzander had told her, but what she hadn't told either of them. She felt good, strong. Stronger than either of them realized. It scared her. Since her first feeding of blood, deep down, not only did this feel right, it felt like this was only the beginning.

Closing her eyes, she inhaled deeply, willing calmness into her soul.

"Well, look who we have here?"

Theodora's eyes snapped open and she looked to her right where Cleo's gleeful voice came from.

"Wasn't I just talking 'bout the best way get her alone?" She asked the six large formidable men flanking her.

With black sunken eyes, pale brittle-looking skin, the same dark cropped hair and dressed in the typical bad guy black, they nodded their reply in unison.

"As luck would have it, here you are all alone. Like a gift from god." She chuckled as they made their way towards her.

Theodora's fight overpowered her flight once more, and she stood to face them.

"What do you want?"

"Well, we really wanted Lyzander. But since I can no longer get to him, I'll settle for you, my queen.

Dead!"

The six men let their fangs drop, confirming what she had suspected. She was now facing six, deadly blood fiend vampires eager to hurt her.

Lyzander! Theodora cried out with her mind.

Cleo lunged forward, throwing a punch at Theodora, moving with deadly vampiric speed.

But instead of making contact, Theodora instinctively turned her face to the side and dodged the punch with ease. Cleo threw a right but she blocked it with her left forearm. She threw a left and she blocked that too before shoving Cleo in the chest with enough force that she flew several feet, landing hard on her ass. Empty glasses smashed on the ground as tables and chairs went flying across the balcony garden.

"But you're a human, how is this possible?" Cleo snarled astounded at her strength.

"How the fuck should I know?" Theodora cried out, staring at her hands in wonder.

"Get her!" Cleo shouted, and the six vampires lurched forward.

What happened next lasted mere seconds.

The first vampire come at her with a sword, slicing it through the air with each step. Managing to dodge his forward thrust, she grabbed his wrist, turning to bodycheck the vampire with the skill of an NHL hockey player. Taking the sword from his hand, she turned to face him, slicing through his neck and taking his head off in one fluid motion.

Blood sprayed out in an arc, raining down on Theodora like a bloody shower before his body turned to ash. Some of the blood got into her mouth and she shivered. It tasted nothing like Lyzander's, but like acid. She was horrified, but it didn't have time to take hold as something came hurtling towards her from her left.

With the sword in her right, she turned swiftly and caught the object midair with her left hand. Looking down she couldn't quite comprehend what she was seeing. She was holding fire. A large flaming ball of red fire. But it wasn't burning her, it didn't hurt. In fact, she couldn't feel a thing.

The vampire who threw it was still moving towards her, but to her, it was as though he was moving in slow motion. She threw it back, hitting him directly in the chest. The red flame engulfed him, incinerating him on the spot and his ashes sprinkled down around where he once stood.

Something slammed into her back but it didn't hurt. Instead, her body was infused with raging power. Intuitively, she knew it was Lyzander. She turned her head and saw that he was brandishing his own Katana.

Cleo and the remaining vampires came at them, biting, kicking and slicing at them with swords, knives and other weapons. Lyzander switched their position, turning Theodora so he could grab Cleo by the throat and shake her in the air like a rag doll. At the same time, he used his sword to fight another vampire who came at him with two blades. Cleo lashed out, trying to get her hands on him and he turned her, using her as a shield, letting the vampire take chunks out of her with his knives.

Theodora kept another vampire at bay with her sword. She was distracted for a split second when a ball of red flames appeared in her left hand, but as another vampire approached, she knew what she had to do. Throwing it at her target, she turned him into a pile of ash.

She took a deep breath and looked around. She could hear Lyzander taking care of those at her back. The balcony was covered in blood and ash. Two bodies lay still, severed and broken on the ground. The rest had long since disintegrated. They were no match for their king and queen.

Cleo was clinging on, gurgling on her own blood as her throat had been partially ripped out by Lyzander. The remaining vampire screamed in pain, his body pumping blood profusely after being separated from all of its limbs.

"You will die." He choked out. "He will send the purebloods...and kill you all for this...the true king knows you exist now." He rasped out to Theodora, giving her a bloody smile. "You will all die." It was the last thing he uttered before Lyzander severed his head, turning him to ash.

Still holding her bloody sword, Theodora walked over to Cleo, who lay in a pool of blood, her arms and legs bent at odd angles and her body cut to ribbons.

With hate filled eyes, she stared up at her queen. "Make...it...quick." Was all she managed to whisper.

Theodora raised her left hand, producing the red flames. "Goodbye, Cleo."

Cleo closed her eyes for the final time.

Lyzander turned Theodora away from the pile of ash, towards him, and raised her head. Breathing heavily and covered in blood, she looked every bit the warrior he needed by his side.

In that moment, he realized exactly what she really was.

"My queen," he whispered in awe.

"What did I just do?" Adrenaline was still pumping through her system but the rational part of her was already trying to push its way back to the forefront.

"You survived."

"I killed them." Disgust was evident in her tone.

"Yes, but in doing so you kept us alive. You were magnificent."

Behind them, a door opened and they turned in unison, ready for battle.

Roman and Sam stepped out onto the balcony, mid conversation. Roman was carrying a large bag of takeaway food while Sam held a stack of napkins and cutlery. They froze, their mouths agape at the sight that greeted them.

Blood and ash covered every surface, including Lyzander, who was stood with his sword raised above his head. Theodora resembled a bloody lady justice, with her sword held in one hand and her burning flame held high in the other.

"What the fuck is that?" Sam almost shouted, gesturing to the fire.

Theodora glanced down at the flames and closed her hand into a fist, dousing the flame. Everyone watched as smoke rose up from her closed fist. When she opened her hand, it was normal once more.

"I was gone for just a minute. A minute! What the hell happened?"

"Are you alright?" Roman asked, worried.

"We are." Lyzander nodded.

"What happened?"

"Vampires." Lyzander stated blandly.

"Bad vampires," Theodora corrected.

"How many?" Roman frowned.

"Seven. Cleo came back to try and kill Theodora but she was no match. It seems my keeper, our new queen, is a siphon."

Roman was unable to hide his shock. "I'm not sure how that is even possible, but you truly are a gift, my queen." He bowed.

"Why? What's a siphon?" Theodora frowned in

confusion.

"Each vampire has their own particular gift." Lyzander explained. "A siphon can draw on the power and gifts of other vampires. Some powers are borrowed and stay with you temporarily, while others will always remain a part of you. To draw on at will."

"How many other siphons are there?"

"Before you, there was only one living siphon still left. Me."

That was it. Theodora couldn't take any more. She was hungry and tired. And after what she had just done, it was too much for her mind to reconcile. A breakdown was imminent.

Sam could see it while Lyzander could feel it through their bond.

Sam took a step forward before remembering the warning about touching her in front of Lyzander and instead, he looked her over. She was pale and covered in blood, looking like she's stepped out of a horror film.

Lyzander took her by the shoulders and turned her towards him. "You need food and rest, Theodora. I will take you and Sam back to the apartments. You can clean up before we leave." He turned to his second-in-command. "Roman, I want the jet ready within the hour. We're going to France. All of us."

"What?" Sam exclaimed.

"Why?" Theodora glanced up at him.

"Because that stupid vampire gave us our first crumb. He was French. He said the purebloods are going to kill us. Who do we know with a connection to France and the purebloods?"

"Gaspard," Roman growled.

"Exactly." Lyzander nodded sharply.

"Purebloods? Is that the same as a natural born vampire?"

He shook his head. "No, they are something else entirely. I'll explain on the way."

"Why do we have to go with you?"

"Because, my dear queen, even though I now know you can take care of yourself, no one will ever get that close to you again. From now on, I'm never letting you out of my sight."

Theodora sighed. "You know what? I'm too tired to give a shit. Come on, Sam. I need a shower." She turned her back on the disarray.

They left the balcony garden, leaving the bloody mess behind for someone else to clean up.

An hour later, they were all safely and comfortably buckled in on Lyzander's jet, France bound. But none of them was prepared for what awaited them.

EPILOGUE

Gaspard, a naturally tall and wide man, felt mighty uncomfortable and restricted in the expensive suit he wore. But he had to look the part every time he came into the city. With his long black hair pulled back into a braid, it was the neatest he was ever going to be.

He walked down the long corridor and knocked once on the frosted glass door. Without waiting for an answer, he entered the familiar office.

For such a large room, there was hardly anything in it. A large mirror on one wall reflected the moonlight streaming in from the ceiling to floor windows while the remaining walls were left bare. The only furniture in the room was a large desk, on which sat a laptop and mobile phone, and two leather back office chairs.

Sitting down, he looked across at the handsome, well-dressed man who occupied the other seat and waited for him to speak.

"Well, that was a disaster." Gaspard sighed in

defeat.

"On the contrary," the man said, with an easy smile.

"What?"

"It went exactly as I had expected."

The man looked to be in his early twenties, but was in fact much older and stronger than Gaspard was. The cold eyes staring back at him practically radiated power, giving his age away.

"But all our soldiers died."

"Of course they did. Well, not all of them died. One or two of them are still waiting for orders. "

"You knowingly sent them to their slaughter." Gaspard smiled back as realisation dawned on him.

"They were going up against the council. There was no way they were going to survive."

"So it was a test?"

"Yes, and I'm thrilled with the results. They were our weaker soldiers and they got close. They almost killed Isaac, which proves just how weak and compliant the council have become. Bowing to humans when we should be ruling over them" He hissed.

"It's time I claimed what is rightfully mine. And when I do, there will be no more hiding in the shadows from these humans. Vampires have always been at the top of the food chain, and it's time we started acting that way again."

"I couldn't agree with you more." Gaspard

nodded.

"Once I've dealt with Lyzander and his precious council, there will be no more suppressing who we really are."

"No more begging donors to part with their blood." Gaspard sneered.

"No. We will take what we want, and the humans will bow to us. This is the way it always should have been and would be, had it not been for Orson."

"If only you'd gotten rid of him sooner before the council took power."

"If only. But no matter. It's time to take power now."

"Won't the council be on alert?"

"Even if they are, they will not stand a chance with your boys by our side."

"You think they are ready?"

"Oh yes, I've been watching them myself."

"What if they're not willing?"

"Then it's your job to make sure they are."

"I won't fail you." He muttered, confident in his own ability.

"Of course you won't, you never do."

"And I never will."

"That is exactly why I chose you to be at my side, Gaspard. You remind me of me." His eyes shone with approval.

"Thank you." Gaspard bowed lightly.

"Here."

The man slid a piece of paper over. On it was the flight details of a private jet heading to France.

"I've called Loic. He will be waiting for you. Go get your boys. It's time to crush the council and take care of that pseudo leader and his brothers once and for all." He chuckled darkly.

* * * *

THE END

Dark Hamlet: Book 1 in the Soul Keeper Series - coming soon.

Thank you so much for reading my book. I'd love to hear what you thought of it. If you enjoyed it that's great, if not let me know why. Please stop buy and leave a review.

Thank you.

RED RIGHT HAND - A PARANORMAL ROMANCE NOVELLA:

Dermott McGuinty intended to be a good man but unfortunately for him the devil had other plans. Dermott is given the opportunity to be the next right hand man to the devil but when an assignment turns out to be the woman of his dreams will he have what it takes to get the job done. If he does what will it cost him in the end?

Available on Amazon:https://amzn.to/2KCqh2G

A STRANGE AFFAIR - AN EROTIC ROMANCE:

She is struggling to fight her dark desires.

He is trying to fight his feelings.

Neither of them can fight their chemistry.

Ellie **Ré** doesn't have time for men. They don't fit in with her career plan. She doesn't engage in flings or one night stands either, it's just not how she was raised. So when Aaron Strange enters her life she's thrown by her sudden dark desires. The feeling of wanting nothing other than to submit to this man terrifies her, but it excites her more. Will she give in to what feels right when she always thought it to be wrong?

Aaron Strange is happy at his new company. He can't get distracted here. He doesn't have time for emotional entanglements. But when he meets Ellie, something about her compels him to get closer. Is it because she refused him? Is it because she surprises him? Is it because he wants to possess her? Aaron finds himself wanting nothing more than to open her eyes to a world of pleasure and desire. But can he convince her to submit to the dark side and not fall for Ellie in the process.

This is a very spicy little Novella with a little humor and a lot of pleasure. Intended for 18 + readers.

Available on Amazon https://amzn.to/2M7HhTg

THE SECRET SIDE OF US
- A CONTEMPORARY ROMANCE:

Will she have the courage to go for who & what she really wants?

When a naive young Lexi leaves everything behind to start a new life in LA she suddenly finds herself caught between two men: Dane a charming American and Ryan a mischievous Italian. Told from the perspective of various characters, this story follows the highs and lows of a vulnerable young woman trying to stick up for herself and follow her heart in a tough, hot city.

Available on Amazon https://amzn.to/2OQGVip

ABOUT THE AUTHOR

Brienne Dubh comes from a performing
background with over 10 years acting

experience. Studying performing arts and theatre at
college she then went on to

university where she studied creative arts. Originally
from England, after a few

years of travelling the world she moved to Ireland
where she currently lives on a homestead with her
husband, two young daughters, ten chickens and a
cat.

*

Connect with Brienne Dubh

Thank you for reading my book I really appreciate
you taking the time out. If you

enjoyed it please take a moment to leave a review!
Here are my social media coordinates:

Check out my site:

www.briennedubhauthor.com

Follow me on twitter: twitter.com/BrienneDubh

Friend me on facebook:
www.facebook.com/BrienneDubh?ref=stream

or email briennedubh@gmx.com